"You can't hold week—"

"Wanna bet?" A wicked grin curved Grey's mouth as he slowly moved toward Mariah. "I kinda like the sound of you being my captive, at my mercy...."

She held up her hand to ward him off. "I'm not staying at this cabin with you. Give me the keys to the Jeep," she ordered.

"Search me for them," he dared, holding his arms wide to give her access to every inch of him. "If you find them, we'll go."

The only thing she'd find would be a body to die for, and a man who'd enjoy every minute of the frisking. Mariah sighed in frustration. "Why are you doing this?"

More quickly than she could anticipate, he slid his hand around the back of her head and brought her mouth to his. He summed up his answer in a deep, emotion-filled kiss that left her clinging to him.

When he finally lifted his head, she stared up at him in a dazed fog, a willing prisoner.

"*That's* why I'm doing this," he said, his eyes blazing with heat. "Now, I assume there are no more arguments?"

Dear Reader,

Every man has a weakness, and for Grey Nichols, it's
Mariah Stevens. He's crazy about her, and he can't
imagine his life without her in it. Never has he met a
woman who complements him so perfectly…and he
decides there's only one thing left for him to do—
propose that she move in with him.

As far as heroes go, Grey is as irresistible and
charming as they get. Not to mention gorgeous and
sexy! *I'd* have a hard time resisting his proposition, but
Mariah has strong beliefs. Even though she's head over
heels in love with Grey, she can't accept his cynical
views toward love and marriage. And she certainly
won't settle for anything less than a lifetime
commitment.

Private Pleasures is my first book for Temptation.
It's a thrill for me to be among the many Temptation
authors I've read and loved for years. I hope you enjoy
reading about Mariah's greatest challenge—leading
her reluctant groom to the altar. And the story doesn't
stop there! Next month, Mariah's sister Jade finds a
man who makes her every fantasy come true, in
Private Fantasies, the second part of my two-alarm
BLAZE.

Enjoy,

Janelle Denison

PRIVATE PLEASURES
Janelle Denison

Harlequin Books

TORONTO • NEW YORK • LONDON
AMSTERDAM • PARIS • SYDNEY • HAMBURG
STOCKHOLM • ATHENS • TOKYO • MILAN
MADRID • WARSAW • BUDAPEST • AUCKLAND

To Dad, who has shown me that with hard work and
dedication, I can do or be anything I set my mind to.
To Mom, for your support, encouragement and
unending pride.

To a treasured friend, Jamie Ann Denton,
for more reasons than simple words could ever express.

And as always to my husband, Don, who gives me the
confidence to believe in myself. You are the reason all my
dreams have come true.

ISBN 0-373-25779-1

PRIVATE PLEASURES

Copyright © 1998 by Janelle Denison.

1

MARIAH STEVENS TIPTOED around the shadowy bedroom, quietly picking up her scattered clothes so she wouldn't wake the man sprawled on the huge cherry-wood bed dominating the masculine room. Hunter green bedsheets were tangled in his long, muscular legs, and by sheer luck managed to drape over his hips just enough to cover him modestly. But the rest of his body was bare...gloriously, magnificently bare.

Looking away from that distracting chest and lean belly, she concentrated on her search. In her eight months of dating Grey Nichols she'd seen him naked plenty, but the sight of him never failed to arouse all her feminine instincts. One touch, even a simple, chaste caress, had the ability to melt her heart and body. The scoundrel knew it, too, and used that knowledge to his advantage.

Moonlight spilled into the room from an unshaded window, shimmering off her teal suit skirt and panty hose. She retrieved the items and added them to the neat pile at the foot of the bed, then picked up her slip.

Grey stirred, and she glanced in his direction. He stretched like a big, lazy cat, muscles and sinew rippling with the movement. The sheet dipped low as he reached toward the side of the bed she slept in when she spent the night. His hand grappled with air, her vacant pillow, then fell slack. His sable lashes drifted open and their eyes met. She stilled.

He had the most fascinating eyes. Like chocolate spun with the finest gold. Seductive, warm and altogether too sexy. She remembered thinking when they first met that he had bedroom eyes, the kind that had the ability to undress a woman in a single, sweeping glance, or make a woman shed her inhibitions and undress for him. He'd managed to do both.

A familiar honeyed warmth flowed through her, and she resisted the urge to do exactly what those incredible eyes were asking: take off the shirt she wore and slide back into bed.

The piece of lingerie slithered through her fingers like quicksilver and pooled on the rest of her garments. "Hi," she said.

"Hi, yourself." His voice was a sleepy rumble, his smile pure, unadulterated sin. "What're doin'?"

"Picking up my clothes." Finally spotting her panties by his walk-in closet—how in the world had they gotten clear across the room?—she scooped them up and put them on.

Rolling to his side, he leaned on his elbow and propped his head in his palm, watching her as she bent over. "The view is great, honey, but three hours after the fact isn't the time to start worrying about your clothes being wrinkled."

"I know that." She shot him an exasperated look, tempered by a soft smile. "I need to go."

He glanced at the glowing digital clock on his nightstand, then back at her. "It's past midnight. Stay the night."

"I can't." She disappeared into the bathroom for a moment and returned with a brush she kept in a drawer Grey had given her for her things.

He frowned. "Why not?"

She turned on the brass lamp on the dresser, illuminating the room with a soft glow. Pulling the brush through the tangles in her long, waist-length hair, she met his gaze in the mirror. "I don't have a change of clothes and I have an early appointment with a very important client."

"Let Jade handle the account."

At the mention of her sister and interior design partner, she shook her head. "He specifically asked for me." Separating her hair into three parts, she began braiding the blond strands. "He's a very conservative businessman who wants to redecorate his office. I'm afraid Jade's splashy, offbeat visions would scare him away."

Grey chuckled, the sound low and intimate in the dusky room. "You've got a point. Her clientele does tend to run toward the eccentric."

"That's why we work so well together." Finding an elastic band on his dresser, she tied off the end of her braid and flipped it over her shoulder. "We each have our own style, which gives our clients more variety."

He crooked his finger at her. "C'mere and I'll show you some variety."

"I've got to go, Grey." Regret tinged her voice. "Really."

He sighed heavily. "I hate it when you sneak out on me, you know that, don't you?"

She rolled her eyes at his exaggeration. "I never 'sneak' out on you." Opening one of his drawers, she rummaged through the contents until she found a pair of soft, drawstring sweatpants.

"*Now* what are you doing?"

"Borrowing a pair of sweatpants so I don't have to wear my suit home." She approached the bed, one brow lifted. "Do you mind?"

"Yeah, I mind." Quick as a snap, he manacled her wrist

and tumbled her onto the bed. Quicker, he pinned her beneath the heat and strength of his body. She gasped and stared into dark, predatory eyes fueled with purpose. The sweatpants fell from her fingers and slid to the floor.

"Do you know," he said in a slow, deliberate drawl, "that you look great in my shirt?"

The meltdown began, liquefying her bones. When he wielded that seductive charm of his she couldn't resist him. Didn't want to. It amazed her how tender and playful Grey could be when they were alone, the ruthless, arrogant facade he presented to the rest of the world gone.

"Yeah?" she prompted huskily.

"Umm." He nuzzled her neck while he unbuttoned the shirt in question, his fingers brushing the swell of her breasts. "You look even better wearing nothing at all."

She closed her eyes and automatically arched her neck for his mouth. A shiver of anticipation cascaded down her spine. She had to stop this madness.

"Grey—" His name escaped on a wispy catch of breath.

He lifted his head to stare into her eyes. "You fit perfectly into my life," he murmured.

Her heart skipped a beat. His words were the most intimate declaration he'd ever given her. She'd often wondered about fitting into his life, considering the unconventional way their relationship had evolved—quickly, and with a fiery passion that had both terrified and thrilled her. Grey was like no other man she'd ever known.

He'd pursued her with a single-mindedness, an *I-want-you-in-my-bed* kind of single-mindedness. And still, knowing his intentions, she'd fallen hard for him and his seduction of flowers, dinners and drugging kisses. Then came that fateful night in his office when a kiss had led to a touch, a touch to intimate caresses, shed clothing and

wicked promises. When he'd gently pressed her onto his leather couch and followed her down, she'd lost her heart. Although he'd made her none of the promises she'd longed to hear, she'd been more than willing to make love with him.

Much to her surprise, he hadn't dropped her for another conquest, as was his reputation, she'd learned from a few male colleagues. She didn't know what made her different from all his other brief affairs, but it had never mattered. Being deliriously in love with someone tended to obliterate all reason.

They were good together and very compatible in bed—especially in bed, she thought with a private smile—in business and on a personal level, though she occasionally felt he kept a part of himself distanced from her. A part of his past he'd never shared before. Something emotional and painful. She'd granted him that privacy, hoping in time he'd come to trust her enough to confide in her.

Grey pushed the collar of his shirt off her shoulder, baring her breasts and bringing Mariah back to the present. Dark eyes watched her nipples grow taut in the cool night air. "I hate it when you leave in the middle of the night."

She loved that boyish pout of his. Smiling, she pressed her hands lightly against his chest, reveling in the feel of firm muscle and crisp, curly hair. "I can't help it."

He dragged his gaze back to hers. His serious expression tightened the lines around his eyes and mouth. "I want to wake up to you every day."

She searched his face, seeing a vulnerability that touched a tender chord in her and sped up her pulse. "What are you saying, Grey?"

He pulled in a deep breath. "You know I'll be moving into my new house next week."

"Yes." His "new" house was a breathtaking five-thousand-square-foot custom-built home that sat on a hill overlooking Malibu Beach. She'd spent the past six months consulting with Grey over tile squares, carpet samples, fabric swatches and wallpaper samples, along with selecting all new furnishings for each room. "The decorating was finalized two days ago and furniture should be delivered the beginning of the week. You should be able to move in by Friday. I'd be more than happy to help you box stuff and move it—"

He pressed two fingers against her lips to stop her babbling. "Mariah, there's something very important I want to ask you."

Her stomach flip-flopped, then a batch of butterflies hatched. He looked nervous, more nervous than she'd ever seen him. Beneath her palms, his heart raced. God, she was crazy in love with him, had known after a few months of dating that he was a man she could spend the rest of her life with. She'd been patient with him. Had he finally realized he loved her, too? That marriage was the only logical progression left to their relationship?

She'd waited forever for this moment, when some man would ask her to be his wife. Maybe it sounded a bit corny, but ever since she was a little girl she'd dreamed of getting married and having babies. In all her fantasies, she'd never envisioned Grey proposing in quite this way, but then Grey never did anything conventionally. All at once she was aware of her disheveled state after their evening together, her skin still tingling and glowing from his earlier possession.

Sh. dampened her bottom lip with her tongue. "What is it?"

His intense gaze focused on her face. The stubble lining

his jaw gave him a dark, dangerous edge. "We've been dating for eight months now," he stated, his tone rough.

She smiled, trying to lighten the moment for him and put him at ease. "Longer than you've been with any woman, I do recall you saying."

"True," he agreed, skimming a hand along the curve of her waist to her hip. "I don't want anyone but you. You're everything I've ever wanted. You're intelligent, beautiful, amusing and sexy as all hell."

"Flattery will get you everywhere, Nichols," she teased in a sultry voice. She twined her arms around his neck, feeling languorous and wonderfully exhilarated. "I'm glad you still feel that way."

"I've definitely met my match."

Excitement and anticipation mingled. She shifted restlessly beneath him, wanting to hear those four words that would irrevocably change the direction of her life. "What did you want to ask me, Grey?"

He cleared his throat, hesitated, then, "Will you... I mean, I think we should... Aw, hell," he muttered in frustration.

Seeing how difficult it was for him to propose, she decided to make it easy on him. She placed her hand on his bristly cheek, certain the love she felt for him shone in her eyes. "Yes, Grey," she whispered. "I'll marry you."

He blanched and jerked away from her, a horrified expression transforming his handsome features. "Marry?" The one word choked out of him.

"Yes." She frowned. Had she misunderstood his intentions? More cautiously, she continued. "That is what you were trying to ask me, wasn't it?"

Shaking his head wildly, he moved off the bed faster than a thief escaping a potentially volatile situation. "No!"

Confused, she sat up, pulling the edges of the shirt around her bare breasts. "Then what were you going to ask me?"

He filched the sweatpants she'd taken from his dresser and yanked them on, pulling the drawstring tight around his waist. He paced the floor, his mouth stretched into a grim line.

Feeling foolish that she'd misdiagnosed all the signs pointing toward a marriage proposal, she wrapped her arms around her drawn-up knees to hold herself together. "Grey?" Her voice was as tentative as she felt.

Abruptly he stopped a few feet away from her side of the bed. "I...I want you to move into my new house with me."

Her stomach took a dive off a very steep cliff, taking her heart with it. "Move in with you?" she echoed, praying she'd somehow heard him incorrectly.

He pushed his fingers through his thick, sable hair. "It's a practical arrangement, considering how we virtually live together as it is. Most of the time you stay here, but I'm tired of ping-ponging between both of our condos. And with you living with your sister, we rarely have any privacy at your place."

She stared at the man she loved, trying to claw her way out of the numbing shock of disillusionment fogging her mind. "You...you want to *live* together?"

He breathed a sigh of relief and smiled. "Yes."

She couldn't live with empty promises. Not again. No matter how much she loved him. "No."

He looked taken aback by her reply. "No?"

"No!" Her strength returned on a wave of determination. "I can't live with you, Grey."

"Why not? You know all my bad habits," he said, then added a shrug. "Not that I have many."

She lifted a brow at his arrogant assumption.

"Okay, I have a few habits that are less than desirable," he admitted, "but I'd hardly call squeezing the toothpaste from the middle of the tube a crime. And I know you hate it when I leave my underwear on the floor, but I eventually pick it up."

If they were having this discussion under different circumstances she'd be laughing by now. But that was difficult to do when she felt like crying instead. "This isn't about toothpaste or your underwear, Grey. It's about commitment."

He jammed his hands on his hips, looking offended. "I'm committed to you."

She swallowed the knot in her throat and tasted the awful bitterness of despair. "Not in the way that matters."

"I haven't dated anyone *since* you." She recognized the tight clenching of his jaw. An involuntary action that happened whenever he was losing control of a situation. "Eight months is longer than I've ever lasted in a relationship. Doesn't any of that matter?"

She smoothed her hand over the cool sheets, unable to lie to him. "Yes, it matters." But she wanted, and needed, *more*.

He sat on the edge of the bed next to her, searching her gaze for answers. "If it matters, then why can't you move in with me?"

Her one experience living with a man had given her a clearer perspective of what she wanted. This time she wasn't going to settle for less than full measure. "Because the day I move in with someone is the day I'm wearing a wedding ring. *That's* the kind of commitment I'm talking about. A forever kind of commitment. A total commitment shared by two people in love."

He rubbed his forehead with his fingers, his expression

reflecting his misery. "You knew I wasn't looking for marriage when we got involved, that I don't intend to get married. *Ever.*"

"Yes, you did say that, but I kept hoping your feelings would change."

"My feelings *have* changed," he stated emphatically. "I care for you more than I've cared for *anyone* in my entire life."

"I'm touched. Truly I am," she said, aching deep inside for something she knew would never be. "But it's not enough. Not anymore."

"It was enough a month ago, a week ago, a *day* ago," he pointed out, his voice rising in frustration.

"I love you, Grey." It wasn't the first time she'd said those words to him, yet the sudden terror in his eyes was as fresh and raw as the first time she'd declared her emotions to him.

He blinked away the panic and forcibly regained his composure. Grasping her hand, he brought it to his lap and held it gently. "I know you do, sweetheart—"

"Do you love me?"

His face paled, and the fingers stroking her palm stilled. "I've never asked another woman to live with me."

She managed to laugh. "I guess I should consider it an honor, but that's not what I asked you."

Dropping her hand, he stood and prowled around the room, his body tense. She watched him, trying to understand the perimeters of their relationship. Grey had never been one to express his emotions verbally; she'd learned that over their months together. He'd never told her he loved her, but she knew what they had together was special—special enough to base a future on. And sometimes, when he looked at her a certain way, she was positive he

loved her, whether he verbally expressed the emotion or not.

"I don't know if what I feel for you constitutes as 'love,'" he said, shooting major holes in her theory. "Hell, Mariah, I don't even believe in love."

She hadn't known that. The knowledge hurt and saddened her. All her life she'd been surrounded by people who loved her, family who openly expressed their feelings and emotions. She wondered how she could have been so blind to this cynical side to Grey, how she could have believed he just needed time to fall in love with her.

"People grow to care for one another, and I care for you deeply," he went on. "Love is an illusion, a pretty word for something that doesn't really exist."

"That's not true," she argued. "My parents are in love, and they've been happily married thirty-nine years."

He shot her a skeptical look. "Your parents are in the minority. My mother claims to have been in 'love' four, no five times, and has been divorced just as many times." He shook his head in disgust. "If that's what love and marriage is all about, I don't want any part of it."

Mariah digested that. She didn't have to scratch much deeper than the surface of that speech to realize he'd had a crummy childhood. He'd never told her much about his family, just that he'd been an only child, and that his father had died when he was thirteen. Every time she'd ask, he'd brushed off the subject and gone on to another. Now she knew why. She wanted to know more about his parents, his childhood. But she really didn't think now was the time to discuss family relations.

Grey picked up his briefs lying on the floor and dropped them into the dark green hamper just inside the bathroom. "Why is marriage suddenly so important to you, Mariah?"

"It's *always* been important." Heavyhearted, she slid off the bed, instinctively knowing that after tonight they would never be the same. How could they be when they both had different visions for their futures?

He blocked her way to her clothes, his five-inch advantage and his dark scowl making him appear imposing. "Marriage wasn't important when you moved in with Dale Simmons."

She cringed at the reminder of her previous catastrophic relationship. "That's why I won't make *that* mistake again. It's too convenient living with someone. All the luxuries of a marriage without the emotional obligations. I want total commitment, Grey. All or nothing. And we've been together long enough, without living together, to know whether or not a marriage would work."

He obviously didn't think one would, but then again, she'd just recently discovered that he didn't have much faith in the institution of marriage.

She attempted to step around him, but he blocked her path again. His intense gaze captured hers. "Did you love him?" he asked abruptly.

She didn't need to ask who he meant. "Yes."

"Did he love you?"

"Yes." At least for a while she'd known Dale loved her.

"The guy fooled around with other women behind your back!" he said, shaking his head incredulously. He grabbed her arms, his grip gentle but firm. "Doesn't that make you think, even for a moment, that love isn't all that it's cracked up to be?"

It had been poor judgment on her part. That, and Dale had strung her along with empty promises she'd been too naive to see through. At thirty-two she'd like to think she was wiser than she'd been at twenty-six.

"That experience has made me cautious about the men

I date, but not totally against a lifelong commitment. I want that, Grey, and I want that with you, not the convenience of living with someone then deciding you want something better."

Grey dropped his hands back to his sides, feeling more defeated than he had in his entire life. She was asking for something he didn't have in him to give. He could tell her exactly what she wanted to hear, but if anything, their relationship had always been based on trust and honesty, and he refused to taint it with lies. And there was no way he'd let her believe he had any intentions of getting married. To anyone. Ever.

"I...I can't, Mariah," he whispered.

Tears welled up in her eyes, but she held her chin high. "Then I think we need to start seeing other people." She skirted past him.

He turned just in time to see her swipe a tear from her cheek. His stomach twisted into a gigantic knot. He never wanted to hurt her. He couldn't give her what she wanted, but he didn't want to lose her, either, no matter how selfish it seemed.

"I don't want to see anyone else, Mariah," he said, as if that might change her mind about them. About staying. About moving in with him.

Her back to him, she shrugged out of his shirt and slipped on her bra and blouse, then faced him while doing up the buttons. "Neither do I, but I don't want to invest anything more into a relationship that won't go any farther than this. I want a husband, Grey, and children. Do you want children?"

Her question caught him off guard. They'd never discussed kids before, but then he'd had no reason to. He'd always known they'd never be a part of his future, and

that was the end of that discussion for him. Cut-and-dried. No compromise.

"That's what I thought." Weary resignation laced her voice. She stepped into her teal skirt and shimmied it up those long, slender legs he'd found so enticing when they'd first met. Once they'd slept together, those limbs had become an endless source of fascination for him.

"You don't want children, do you?" she asked, an odd catch to her voice.

He dragged a hand over his jaw, despising the old, painful childhood memories creeping up on him. Memories he wanted to remain dead and buried. "I'm too old to be a father."

Her gaze captured his. He was skirting the truth, and the shrewd look in her eyes told him she knew it, too. "Too old or too scared?"

"What's that supposed to mean?" he automatically responded, even as he mentally cursed her perception.

She gave a one-shoulder shrug and slipped into her sling-back pumps. "Being a parent is a scary proposition."

Caustic laughter escaped him. "Yeah, well, I'm afraid I didn't have a great role model growing up, therefore parenthood holds little appeal for me."

"I understand," she said softly as she gathered up the underthings she hadn't put on.

She didn't understand, not really, he thought a little desperately. And he didn't know how to explain emotions he hadn't thought about in over twenty years. An unhealthy bitterness toward a father who'd taken out his grudges on a little boy he'd resented from the start. And resentment toward a mother who'd been too afraid to risk her husband's contempt to protect her child from the

emotional and verbal degradation Aaron Nichols had dished out.

No, Mariah would never understand, not when she'd been raised in a healthy atmosphere with traditional, honest values. Hell, he wouldn't know honorable family morals if they slapped him in the face.

A crushing pressure banded his chest. All his adult life he'd worked hard, his drive and ambition an asset to the small security company he'd built from scratch into a large corporation. He'd learned to wield control, manipulate situations to his advantage and depend on no one but himself. There was nothing he wanted that he hadn't been able to acquire.

Except now, with Mariah. He found it ironic that the one thing he wanted most he couldn't purchase with the millions his business turned over in a year's time. Mariah, it seemed, was priceless.

She turned to him, her eyes a misty blue. "I think it's best if we just end things now."

He didn't move, though his hands balled into tight fists at his sides. "Just like that, it's over?"

"We want different things from a relationship. That's obvious now. There's no sense in going any further." She took a shaky breath. "Goodbye, Grey."

He watched her walk out of his bedroom and his life, listening to the front door click behind her. He sank back onto the bed, an empty, bleak feeling consuming him. He'd spent the majority of his life alone, but he'd never felt so desolate until that very moment.

"Mariah, how long do you intend to mope around?"

Mariah glanced up from the evening news to her sister, Jade, who stood next to the couch with her hands on her skinny hips. She wore a tight leopard-skin top that

hugged her curves and black spandex pants that disappeared into a pair of black leather boots. Her short golden brown hair was teased into a full style and today, thanks to the modern inventions of colored contact lenses, her eyes were a deep violet hue.

"I don't mope," Mariah mumbled. Tucking her legs under her on the couch, she wrapped her old chenille robe around her and reached for the bowl of frozen grapes on the end table. She popped one into her mouth and chewed.

"Correction. You never used to, until a week ago." Jade waved a hand in the air, and the stack of bangle bracelets on her arm tinkled with the gesture. "God, Mariah, you won't even let me erase Grey's answering machine messages because you want to hear his voice. If you haven't noticed, we've run out of tape."

Mariah chewed on another grape. "I'll buy a new one if you'll just leave me alone."

"No way. Somebody's gotta pull you out of this blue funk you're in. Just look at you," she said, shaking her head in disgust. "You're a mess. You only leave the condo to go to work, and even then you just stare off into space. And for goodness' sake, you can't live on frozen grapes alone."

She bit into another icy piece of fruit. "Why not?"

Jade gave an exasperated sigh. "I've never seen you like this before. Not even after you and Dale split up."

Her breakup with Dale had been inevitable, she'd seen that toward the end of their relationship. But with Grey the end had come so suddenly, without any warning. She loved him more than any man she'd ever had a relationship with, but in the end that hadn't been enough—for either of them. She stuffed three more grapes into her mouth.

"Riah," Jade said gently as she sat beside her sister, "even Mom and Dad are concerned about you. Especially Dad. You know how he gets when someone hurts one of his little girls. He was ready to pick up one of his shotguns and pay Grey a visit."

Mariah's head jerked up. "Tell me you're joking."

Jade shrugged, a smile tipping her mouth. "He was just feeling a little protective. He really liked Grey. We all did, and I think he had his hopes set on a wedding. And a grandchild."

Mariah groaned at her father's relentless pursuit to see his daughters married. And his continual reminder that they hadn't managed to give him any grandchildren to bounce on his knee before his arthritis got too bad. "That's not going to happen anytime soon, at least not with Grey. 'Wedding' and 'children' aren't in his vocabulary."

"If that's the case, it's time to move on to new and better adventures."

She shuddered at the thought of dating again, of trying to find someone who shared the same interests and had the same goals. Someone caring, confident, yet sensitive when it counted. Sexy didn't hurt, either, with sable hair and drown-in-them-forever brown eyes. Too late, she realized, she'd just described Grey.

"I don't want to move on," she said woefully.

Compassion softened Jade's expression. "Riah, no man is worth all this self-destruction. Take it from me. I know firsthand."

Yes, she did, Mariah thought, putting the half-eaten bowl of grapes aside. After a very rocky relationship had nearly stripped her of all confidence, Jade had pulled herself from the depths of despair and emerged as a whole new person.

Jade was right. She was wallowing in self-pity, and it

changed nothing. It made her feel a little better, but it didn't alter the empty, lonely feeling inside her. No, she didn't think that would go away for a long, long time.

Taking a shaky breath, she met her sister's caring gaze. "Oh, Jade, I don't know what to do. I miss him so much it hurts. I almost don't care if he won't marry me, just so I can be with him. But then I know we'll eventually break up again, and I'll have to suffer all over."

"I know it's hard, hon," Jade said, patting her knee. "I think what you need to do is get out and meet new men so you can forget about Grey."

She pleated the end of her robe's sash. "I wish it was as easy as that."

"It is."

Mariah frowned, skeptical of the sudden enthusiastic sparkle in Jade's eyes. "It is?"

"Yep." She grinned. "First, we're going to get you a whole new look."

Mariah gulped. "We are?"

Jade nodded. "A head to toe makeover." Picking up a long strand of Mariah's blond hair, she eyed the length critically. "Have you ever thought of trying a new hair-style, maybe cutting it shorter?"

Once, right after she'd met Grey. But when she'd mentioned it to Grey he'd balked at the suggestion, claiming how much he loved her silky long hair. Gently, but firmly, she pulled her hair from her sister's clutches. "No," she lied.

"Too bad. A shorter cut would look awesome on you." Grasping Mariah's chin between thumb and forefinger, she tilted her head up for her inspection. "You've got great cheekbones that you never take advantage of. Ever thought of colored contacts? Green would be stunning."

Mariah pulled her chin back, her lips pursed. "Absolutely not."

"Okay, okay," Jade said, relenting. "But we'll definitely have to spruce up that wardrobe of yours."

"What's the matter with my clothes?" Mariah reached for the bowl of grapes.

Jade caught her sister's hand midstretch and placed it back in her lap. "Your suits are blasé, and the dresses you wear are too conservative. You've got a great figure, Mariah, and lots of cleavage. Display it to your advantage."

Mariah pulled the lapels of her robe higher around her neck.

"And I've seen that dreadful cotton underwear you wear." Jade feigned a loud yawn. "Bor-ing."

"It's comfortable," Mariah said, feeling silly that she had to defend her choice of underwear to her sister.

Jade dismissed her with a wave of her bangled arm. "Trust me, silk feels much better against your skin, and it makes you feel sexy and feminine. It'll boost your sagging spirits."

Mariah was doubtful that a change in lingerie would make her heartache go away but at the moment, looking down at herself in a frumpy robe and socks with holes in them, feeling sexy did hold a certain appeal. "Okay. When do we start this makeover?"

"This weekend. Saturday we'll visit Pierre, my hairdresser, just to trim up the ends of your hair," she assured Mariah when she started to protest. "Then we'll spend the rest of the day getting pampered—facials, manicure, pedicure, massage. The works."

Mariah felt a smile coming on, and gave into the urge to let it spread across her face. "Sounds like an...interesting day."

"Oh, but that isn't all." Sitting back, she rested an arm

across the back of the couch and crossed her long legs, her face wreathed in excitement. "Sunday we spend shopping for your new wardrobe, and in between all this we're gonna clean your room of any traces of Grey. Last, but certainly not least, we're going manhunting at Roxy's Nightclub."

"*Manhunting?*" Mariah's voice squeaked.

"For a new boyfriend." She leaned closer and gave Mariah a dazzling smile. "For *you*."

Letting Jade organize her closet and makeup drawer was one thing, but she didn't trust her sister with her personal life. "I don't want a new boyfriend."

"You don't think you do, but hey, life does go on, and as Dad puts it, he's not getting any younger." She pressed a hand with long red nails against her chest. "I certainly don't have any plans to tie the knot any time soon, so that makes you Dad's only hope. Do you remember Richard Sawyer?"

The switch in subjects threw Mariah off-kilter. "You mean the lawyer who came to see you about a consultation on redecorating his office?"

"That's the one. Tall, blond, rich, with a great body," she recited breezily. "Well, when he was in a couple of weeks ago to sign his contract he asked about you," she said, tapping her knee with a fingernail. "He sounded very interested, if you know what I mean."

She'd been so completely Grey's—heart, body and soul—that the thought of another man touching her, even holding her hand, bothered her. "I don't know, Jade—"

"Tell you what," Jade cut her off with a wink. "I'll tell him you're recently uninvolved and very available, and we'll let nature take its course."

Mariah rubbed her forehead. She couldn't mourn Grey forever. There would come a time when she'd have to cut

her losses and move on and date other men. Her heart rebelled, but logically she knew that was the only smart thing to do. Because, ultimately, she wanted a husband and children, and she couldn't do that without a mate.

She sighed in resignation. "Okay, set me up."

Jade clapped her hands gleefully. "Let the new Mariah emerge!"

2

STANDING IN THE LOBBY of the huge glass-and-chrome building where Grey's company, Nichols' Security Systems, had its offices, Mariah waited for one of the three elevators to make its way back to the main floor. It was after five on a Wednesday, and except for the guard on duty and an occasional business-suited man, the lobby seemed deserted. She would have preferred a swarm of people and a fast elevator to keep her mind off her final mission to sever all ties with Grey.

Pulling in a deep calming breath, she replayed the pep talk her sister had given her over breakfast. While Jade had eaten two bowls of cereal, a muffin and half a grapefruit, she'd counseled Mariah on how to finalize her split with Grey and get on with her life. At the time her advice sounded so simple and easy to execute. Now she wanted to hightail it out of there, go home, curl up in her ratty old robe—not the new satin-and-lace one Jade had coerced her into buying—and eat a bowl of frozen grapes.

Ping. The elevator doors opened with a soft, welcoming whoosh. Butterflies swarmed in her empty stomach, increasing her nervousness about seeing Grey again after two weeks apart. Two weeks of pure torture—no appetite, sleepless nights and a continual ache near the vicinity of her heart. God, she didn't think the horrible pain would ever ease.

Blinking back a surge of tears, she clutched a 4 × 6

gift-wrapped package in one hand and a paper sack in the other and stepped into the elevator. She pressed the button for the fourteenth floor before she could change her mind. The doors closed silently, cocooning her in the mirrored cubicle.

She stared at her reflection in the mirror across from her. The woman reflected back was still a virtual stranger to Mariah, but she was slowly growing accustomed to her new look. And liking it. With Jade and Pierre's coaxing, she'd allowed the master hairdresser to shear her hair into a sleek, shoulder-length bob that curled under at the ends and softened her features. Wispy bangs flattered the simple style and drew attention to her wide blue eyes and the high cheekbones her sister seemed to envy.

She wondered what Grey would think of her new look and the radical change in her choice of clothing. Not that she cared, she resolutely reminded herself.

The elevator stopped on the seventh floor to pick up an executive who rode the lift to the tenth floor and exited, leaving Mariah alone once again. This time when she caught her reflection, a memory leapt into her mind, vivid and provocative. She'd been alone with Grey in this very elevator, on their way to the ground level after spending a few hours in his office discussing color schemes for the library in his new house. At the ninth floor he'd punched the stop button, bringing the elevator to a whining halt.

Mariah closed her eyes against the erotic recollection, but her mind ruthlessly brought that encounter into sharp focus. In her mind's eye she could see Grey moving toward her, a shameless, sexy gleam in his gaze. He'd pressed her against the mirrored wall and skimmed her skirt up her thighs to her hips, then hooked his fingers into the top of her pantyhose.

She'd gasped as he peeled her pantyhose and panties

down her legs in one smooth motion. "Grey, what are you doing?" she asked, even as she obediently stepped from her shoes and lingerie for him.

He tossed the intimate apparel aside, his smile wicked. Unclasping her hair, he dropped the pearl clip onto the plush carpeting and threaded his fingers through the strands, arranging the wavy ends over her shoulders. "I want you."

Her body swelled with heat and desire, but what little modesty Grey hadn't stripped her of kept her from completely surrendering. "We can't do this in here!"

Her shocked tone seemed to amuse him and fire his own passion. He pressed his hips to hers, his erection rock hard and insistent between them. "Sure we can, sweetheart." He brought his mouth to her ear, his tongue touching the sensitive shell as he whispered, "It's late, and there are two other elevators. No one will miss this one for a little while. We don't even have to get undressed all the way."

His hands explored beneath her skirt again, and he touched her intimately, his fingers finding her wet, sleek and ready for him. He groaned into the side of her neck.

"Oh, Grey!" Her knees buckled, but the weight of his body held her upright. She bit her lip to keep from crying out.

He stroked her, and she rewarded him with a whimper and a plea. He lifted his head, his eyes dark as he watched her changing expression. "This is a fantasy I've had about you a million times. Every time I ride alone in these elevators I think of being in here with you. Alone. Like this. Indulge me."

She had. He'd unbuttoned her blouse and pulled the cups of her bra down, so her breasts sprang free for his pleasure.

"This is..." Her breath caught as his lips closed over a swollen nipple.

"Decadent? Erotic?" he said in between kisses and long, slow laps of his tongue.

"Yes," she hissed, unable to ignore the thrill of excitement his seduction evoked. Letting her head fall back and her body melt for him, she tangled her fingers in his hair. When he finally knelt in front of her, she trembled in anticipation.

"It's gonna get a whole lot better," he promised huskily. His mouth, warm and damp, skimmed the inside of her thigh. "Watch in the mirrors before they start to steam."

She had, and the things he'd done to her had taken her beyond anything she'd ever experienced. They'd made love in the elevator not once, but twice, each time wild and searing in its intensity.

Mariah groaned, remembering every erotic word he'd whispered, the slide of his mouth and hands on her body and the desperate way she'd clung to him when he'd finally thrust deep inside her....

"Ms. Stevens? Are you okay?" a distant, feminine voice queried. "Ms. Stevens?"

Mariah blinked her eyes open, horrified to find the elevator doors wide-open to the reception area and Grey's secretary, Jeanie, looking at her oddly. The other woman held an attaché case in one hand and her purse slung over her shoulder as if she were leaving for the evening.

The elevator doors started to close and Jeanie stopped them with a quick hand. "Ms. Stevens?"

Mariah snapped out of her haze with a firm mental shake. "I'm sorry, Jeanie, I must have been daydreaming." Stepping from the lift, she held up the paper bag and package in her hands. After that arousing trip down

memory lane she just wanted to leave Grey's things at the front desk and bolt. She was certain she couldn't face him without falling apart or throwing herself at him. "I just wanted to drop off a few things of Grey's."

Jeanie hurried to the receptionist's desk and set her attaché down. "Let me ring Grey." She reached for the phone.

"That's not necessary, Jeanie," Mariah hastened to assure her. "I'll just leave these things here at the front desk, and you can give them to him after I leave."

Jeanie shook her head adamantly. "He'd be upset with me if I didn't tell him you were here, and it takes very little to set him off these days. He's been such a grouch lately," she confided in a low voice. But there was affection for her boss in her tone, and understanding, too. "I have strict instructions to notify him immediately if you call, so I'm sure the same applies if you stop by."

Mariah liked Jeanie, and she certainly didn't want to put the woman's job in jeopardy. Grey was fair to a fault, but she'd seen his temper once with an obnoxious subcontractor and didn't want to be responsible for Jeanie having to face his wrath for disobeying his orders.

So she waited anxiously as Jeanie picked up the receiver and pressed the intercom button.

"Grey, Ms. Stevens is here." She paused, then said, "No, I don't mind staying until you receive the call from Frank Weisman. I'll send her on back."

Jeanie hung up the phone and gave Mariah an apologetic look. "You know the way."

Mariah nodded and forced herself down the long blue carpeted corridor to Grey's office. With every step she took her nerves increased. Her palms grew damp and her heart pounded in her chest. Stopping at the thick double doors to his office, she dragged in a fortifying breath, de-

termined to get through this visit as quickly as possible and leave with her pride and emotions intact.

She entered the large, spacious room and Grey immediately stood from behind a desk cluttered with papers, files and a computer screen reflecting an estimate spreadsheet.

"You haven't returned my calls," he blurted accusingly.

She cringed guiltily. Stopping just inside the office, her heart gave a giant, yearning leap. He looked awful, she thought, unable to recall a time she'd seen him so weary and worn-out. His dark hair was mussed as if it had been repeatedly finger-combed and his face looked gaunt. Shadows of exhaustion lined his eyes. He wore a pair of navy slacks and a beige shirt with navy pinstripes, the sleeves cuffed to expose his strong forearms.

Resisting the urge to go to him, to help chase away the misery in his golden brown eyes, she set the bag on the chair in front of his desk, and rested the wrapped package against a small end table.

"I didn't return your calls because I knew I was going to see you in person." Why had that sounded so much better when Jade had coached her?

"Dammit, Mariah, this is crazy. I was hoping you'd come to your senses about us, but..." He frowned at her, then a horrified expression twisted his features. He shot around the desk so fast she didn't have a chance to react before he stood in front of her, gaping. "What in the *hell* did you do to your hair?" His voice was a small roar.

Self-consciously she touched the bobbed ends, trying to dismiss the momentary pang of regret she felt. She couldn't live her life for Grey when he was no longer a part of it, she reminded herself.

She squared her shoulders. "I cut it." She sounded

strong and self-assured, like a woman in control. So why didn't she *feel* that way?

"Obviously," he said dryly.

He was looking at her hair like she'd cut off an arm instead. All at once she remembered the way he used to wind the long strands in his fists and gently tug her head back for his kiss, or the way he'd go wild when her hair would cascade over his body whenever he urged her to be the aggressor.

Meeting his smoldering gaze, she realized he was thinking the same things. She bit her bottom lip and looked away. Jade had promised her today's final goodbye would be a "piece of cake." Her sister had lied. Seeing him again and knowing she could never have him hurt worse than the original breakup.

Grey swore beneath his breath, trying to figure out why she'd shear her long, silky hair when she knew how much he loved it. To spite him? No, she wasn't the type. And then it dawned on him.

His gaze narrowed. "Jade had something to do with your hair, didn't she?"

Her mouth pursed in irritation. "Of course not."

Liar, he thought, absorbing other changes he hadn't noticed when she'd first walked in; he'd been too caught up in venting his frustration that she'd been avoiding him for two weeks.

His gaze zeroed in on the cleavage showing where the buttons on her silky white blouse stopped. Mariah's breasts were a generous handful but she'd never been one to display them to their full advantage, choosing instead to wear blouses that adequately covered her or buttoned to the throat. Only *he'd* known how full and perfect those breasts were, and he'd liked it that way.

Through the thin material of her blouse he glimpsed

something lacy that shaped her breasts and disappeared into the waistband of her skirt. One of those teddy things, he guessed, his blood heating at the thought of Mariah trading in her practical underwear for sexy stuff—the kind that incited a man's imagination when they realized a woman was wearing it. The kind that men would spend an inordinate amount of time fantasizing about unwrapping, layer by layer, to discover all the secrets that lay beneath.

He dropped his gaze lower, and his jaw tightened right along with the rest of his body. Her skirt was at least four inches shorter than her normal knee-length. Usually she reserved black stockings for special occasions, yet had donned them with her casual outfit. As a whole, she appeared subdued, sophisticated and damned sexy.

"I don't think I've ever seen you wear a miniskirt before." He would have remembered. Oh, man, would he have. Raw possessiveness ripped through him, and he had the barbaric inclination to nail any man who dared ogle her...like he was.

She shrugged, obviously having no idea what wearing a short skirt that flirted so enticingly around her thighs could do to a man's mental health. And those heels... Christ, they made her legs seem endless. His temperature spiked ten degrees, and a hundred erotic fantasies sprang to mind.

She had no right to look so fresh and sassy, not when he felt and looked like death warmed over. The aggravation of the past fourteen days came to a head. "This new 'look' of yours was Jade's idea, wasn't it? The hair, your clothes," he said, gesturing to each. "Next time I see you your eyes will be purple!"

She sighed and moved away, toward the bank of win-

dows overlooking Century City. "I didn't come here to discuss my sister, my haircut or my choice of clothes."

"Or lack thereof," he muttered, rubbing a hand over his jaw.

She shot him a look over her shoulder. "Grey, please don't make this any more difficult than it already is. I don't want to fight. In fact, I'd like us to be...friends."

"Friends?" He stared incredulously. Dammit, he didn't want a casual, platonic relationship with her! Not after experiencing how good it could be between them. She complemented him so perfectly, and he'd given her more than he'd ever given any woman.

Everything except the two things she claimed to need and he'd never put much faith in: love and marriage. It was a destructive combination he had no desire to be a part of.

He shoved that thought from his mind. "After everything we've meant to each other, everything we've done and shared, you want to revert to being friends?"

"Yes. I'd like to think we're adult enough to maintain a friendship."

"I don't want to be just your friend, Mariah." He strode toward her and grasped her hands, looking deeply into her eyes. "I want to be your lover. I want it to be the way it was between us."

"And I want marriage and babies."

The mere words made him cringe, which he knew she saw.

Regret clouded her expression and she withdrew her hands from his. "I want you to know I'm seeing someone else."

The thought of another man touching her made him feel violent. "Great," he muttered. "Just great." Stomach churning, he fished into his pocket for the roll of antacids

that had become his constant companion the past two weeks. He popped two into his mouth and ground them with his teeth.

"I think you should, too."

He laughed harshly. "How can I when every woman I look at doesn't even come close to comparing to you? Dammit, Mariah, I miss you."

Reciprocating words leapt into her gaze but she said nothing. He silently cursed her willpower while he had absolutely none when it came to her.

He paced the carpet in front of the windows. "I can't sleep at night, can't concentrate during the day and I eat antacids by the case and I hate the damned things! I've been a bear to be around, too. Just ask Jeanie."

She folded her arms over her chest, drawing his gaze to the cleavage spilling from the opening in her blouse. Damn. He resisted the impulse to unbutton her blouse and discover exactly what she was wearing beneath.

"I'm sorry," she said softly.

Stopping abruptly in front of her, he dragged his eyes back to her face. "You should be. It's your fault, you know. I can't let you go. You're with me every second of the day, and at night..." He touched her cheek, letting her imagination take over.

Her breath caught in her throat. Grasping his wrist, she pulled his hand away. "Grey, stop."

"Why? It's the truth." He was wearing down her resistance, could see her fighting against what she truly wanted. Pressing on before he lost his advantage, he stepped closer until their clothes brushed. She tried to take a step back, but a wingback chair stopped her retreat. He didn't touch her, but he planned to....

In a low, husky voice, he continued. "Every night I go to bed thinking of you. I dream of you. And when I wake

up in the morning I'm hard and aching. I always reach for you but you're not there anymore."

The pulse at the base of her throat fluttered, and when she breathed in, the swell of her breasts quivered. "Being apart is just as difficult for me."

"Is it?" Bracing his hand on either side of the chair behind her, he trapped her within his arms. He wasn't taking any chances of her bolting before he was done. "Do you wake up the same way? Wanting me?" Her darkening gaze said what her mouth wouldn't. Dipping his head, he pressed his lips against her ear and continued the mutual torment. "And when you realize I'm not there, do you close your eyes and imagine my hands and mouth on you, touching and stroking you in that special way that makes you come apart for me?"

A tiny groan escaped her, and she pressed her hands to his chest. Her touch seared him, aroused him, thrilled him. The front of his slacks grew uncomfortably snug, but he kept a tight rein on his needs.

"You don't play fair, Nichols," she said on a wispy catch of breath.

He was ruthless when it came to what he wanted, in business, in pleasure and now with Mariah. Inhaling deeply her sweet, feminine scent, he pulled back and met her gaze. She looked dazed, flushed and achingly beautiful. Under different circumstances he would have taken her right then and there. Under different circumstances she would be begging him to. But he was close to getting what he wanted...her complete surrender, body *and* soul.

"My offer still stands," he said.

A little frown marred her brows, and the passionate haze cleared from her eyes. "To move in with you?"

"Yes."

She made a sound of disgust and gave him a shove,

hard enough for him to take a step back and for her to slip out from between him and the chair. "Then my answer is the same."

"It doesn't have to be this way," he said, his voice rising in frustration. "We were perfectly happy until..." Clamping his teeth, he shoved his hands into his pockets and fiddled with the roll of antacids.

"Until what?" She ran a hand through her short hair, and the silky strands bobbed back into place. "Until I realized you didn't and couldn't love me? Until marriage was mentioned and I realized we were looking at our relationship from two different perspectives?" Angry hurt filled her expression. "I can't just make my feelings about getting married and having a family go away, Grey. I want the security of a lifelong commitment with a man who loves me as much as I love him, and I want babies before I'm too old to enjoy them. And I don't want to waste another year or two loving you when I know I'll eventually have to move on."

Her argument was solid. As solid and impenetrable as a brick wall. But with enough patience and persistence, could it be torn down? Grey wondered. Persistence was the reason he was a successful businessman with a multimillion dollar corporation. However, patience wasn't one of his strong suits. But for her, he'd discipline himself.

"I don't ever remember you being so stubborn before," he said, forcing a teasing tone when he felt jagged and torn inside. "Jade got anything to do with that?"

She laughed, the sound strained. "No, I've always been stubborn when it comes to something I believe in. Besides, you're just as stubborn when it comes to your own beliefs about marriage and love."

"With good reason." He strolled to the windows and stared out at the smog hovering over the tall buildings

dominating the city. Grey had witnessed his father hurl insults at his mother and had been the focus of many verbal attacks himself. The man had blamed a mere child for trapping him in a loveless marriage. All of these things had left a lasting impression on Grey.

The lessons he'd learned had proved invaluable through the years, in dealing with the many stepfathers who'd traipsed through his life, in business and his personal life. He'd always steered clear of forming emotional attachments and instead focused on work and the acceptance of his colleagues. In business, at least, he'd gained the respect he'd never received from his father.

"I have no idea what those reasons are," she said from behind him, pulling him from his thoughts. "I've spent eight months with you, and I don't even really know you."

He turned back around. "You know me better than anyone."

"In some ways, yes," she said, strolling around his office and looking at the plaques and awards mounted on the wall. "Physically and on a business level, but emotionally, I'm not quite sure what makes Grey Nichols tick. I know little to nothing about your family, your childhood, what makes you the person you are or why you can't, or won't, commit yourself to marriage and a family." She stopped her wandering and tilted her head at him, regarding him speculatively. "I've learned you're a driven man, but I haven't quite figured out what drives you. I know you built this company from scratch, with no help from anyone. Not because you told me, but because I read it here," she said, pointing to an article from a prestigious business magazine he'd had framed. "Where did that drive come from?"

The answers jammed in his throat, right along with bit-

ter resentments he'd kept buried for years. What Mariah didn't realize is that she knew more about him than he'd ever let any woman close enough to learn. That in itself scared him on an emotional level.

She sighed and propped a hip against the edge of his desk, letting a long, shapely leg dangle. "How can we build a secure relationship when you can't even trust me or talk to me?"

He bristled, feeling raw. "We talk."

"Always about me and my family and my business. We never share things about your life. Or rather, your past." She glanced down at the hands in her lap. Her nails, he noticed, were painted a spring pink color instead of her normal clear polish. "I guess that's why it came as such a shock to learn that you don't believe in love, and you never want to get married. Especially when that's all I've ever wanted."

He smiled, though his heart wasn't in it. "They say opposites attract."

"I hardly think a drastic difference in values is what that quote means."

His fingers curled tight around the pack of Tums. "Then I guess this leaves us at a stalemate, huh?"

Sliding gracefully off his desk, she moved toward the chairs. "How about being friends?"

He figured if that was the only way he could see her, and possibly change her mind about them, then he'd agree to just about anything. "Friends it is," he said, his mood lightening a little. "How about a kiss to seal the pact?"

"How about a gift, instead?" Picking up the large flat package wrapped in burgundy plaid paper, she handed it to him, careful not to let their fingers brush, or anything else for that matter.

"What's this for?" he asked, eyeing the package curiously.

"For you." Her eyes had regained that enthusiastic sparkle he loved. "I bought it when we went to San Francisco two months ago."

He smiled, remembering how he'd surprised her one weekend with plane tickets and reservations at a five-star hotel in San Francisco. "We had a good time, didn't we?"

"Yes, we did," she agreed quietly.

He ran a finger along the smooth edge of the present. "There could be more good times."

Her gaze held his steadily. "No, Grey, not for us."

Strike one, he thought, knowing it would take time to convince her that they belonged together. He turned his attention to the wrapped gift. "How did I miss something so big and bulky on the plane trip back home?"

"I had it mailed." She leaned back against his desk, watching him. "Go on and open it."

He ripped the paper off, revealing a beautiful, expensive painting they'd seen in an exclusive gallery in San Francisco. They'd both been drawn to this painting entitled, *Lover's Cove*. At first glance the picture seemed ordinary; a black, rock-encrusted cove on a secluded stretch of beach, the crystal blue-green water sweeping along the shore. But upon closer observation, and with the gallery owner's shared secret, the shadows on the wall of the cove took the shape of two lovers in an erotic embrace. The painting was beautiful and serene, but intimate for the knowledge of those two lovers who seemed lost in their own private world.

"Thank you," he said, awed by her thoughtfulness when he knew how much she'd wanted the picture for her own. Did she realize he'd never be able to look at the painting and not think of her?

Her smile held genuine pleasure. "It's a housewarming gift for your new home."

"You decorated the place," he said. "You deserve to hang the picture. I've got the perfect spot. In my bedroom."

She saw through his ploy. "I think you can handle hanging a picture on your own."

Strike two. She could hardly blame him for trying. "It was worth a shot." He gently set the picture against the chair. "The place looks great, by the way." *Big and lonely, too, without you there.*

"I'm glad you like it." She looked enormously pleased by his compliment. "If you don't mind, I'd like to send a photographer over to shoot some photos for my portfolio. I'll set up a time when you'll be home."

"That'll be fine." He glanced at his watch. It was nearly six, and he knew he'd never get any work done now. But he didn't want her to leave either. "How about having dinner with me?" he suggested casually. "I can have the Chinese takeout deliver some chow mein and lemon chicken." Her two favorites.

Her gaze glanced off the leather couch against the far wall, then skittered back to him. "You know it would end up being more than just dinner."

True. Every time they'd ever eaten in his office they ended up making love. On the couch. The carpet. His desk. He'd like to think she'd be that weak, but knew better by the determination she'd displayed today.

"I know I'd like for it to be more than that," he admitted with a wicked grin. "But I promise to be on my best behavior."

"You're never on your best behavior." She straightened and smoothed a hand down her very short skirt. "Besides, I can't. I'm meeting someone for dinner at seven."

Jealousy gripped him, demanding another antacid.

She picked up a paper bag and set it on his desk. "Here are the last of your things from my place."

Make that two antacids. "I guess this is it, then, isn't it?"

"Yeah," she whispered, then asked. "Are you still going to my father's sixtieth birthday party?"

"Am I still invited?"

"Of course you are." She picked up her purse and settled the thin strap on her shoulder. "My father has always thought very highly of you."

"Even after our breakup?"

She paused for a moment, as if formulating an adequate response. "Dad was...disappointed to hear we're no longer dating, but he still respects you."

The respect was mutual. He'd met Jim Stevens nearly a year ago, after contracting to install an elaborate security system in the investment firm he owned. Jim was a successful businessman, and it had been obvious that he was very much the family man, as well. He'd boasted about his daughters, and when Grey happened to mention he was building a custom home, Jim had insisted he call his daughter, Mariah, for a consultation on the interior design. Grey had been reluctant—he liked to choose his own women and he certainly didn't like the thought of being "setup"—but in order to maintain Jim's prospering company as one of his accounts, out of courtesy he'd called Mariah. One evening together discussing the design of his house and he'd been a goner.

And now, eight months of bliss was slipping through his fingers. He clung tenaciously to the frayed end of the rope.

"Are we still going to the party together?" That had been the original plan two months ago.

She shook her head. "I don't think that would be such a good idea."

"Why not?"

She dampened her bottom lip with her tongue and looked away. "Because we're not a couple anymore."

The crushing band around his chest tightened. He was feeling desperate...desperate enough to blurt the declaration she thought she needed to hear from him. "Mariah—"

"Grey," Jeanie's voice drifted through the intercom on his desk. "The call from Mr. Weisman that you've been waiting for is on line two."

Damn. He'd forgotten about Weisman. The man was on the verge of signing a two-hundred-thousand-dollar contract, and he was damn hard to get a hold of. "Thank you, Jeanie. I'll take the call and you can leave."

He wanted Mariah to stay, but she was already inching toward the door in those sexy high heels and swaying her skirt enticingly.

"I've got to go, anyway, Grey," she said, gliding across the room, farther and farther away from him. Hand on the doorknob, she paused, blue eyes wide and filled with conflicting emotions. "I guess I'll see you at my father's party."

Two weeks. How was he going to survive another fourteen days without seeing her? Touching her? Talking and laughing with her? Fourteen days of wondering if this other guy she was dating would offer her the two things he couldn't give her.

Any man would be a fool not to.

The roll of Tums snapped in half between his fingers. "Yeah, I'll see you there."

3

"CHRIST, GREY, you look like hell."

Grey glanced up as his good friend Mark Davis slid onto the vacant barstool next to him. "Par for the course," he muttered, taking a gulp of his second scotch of the evening. "I feel like hell."

Monday had always been designated boys' night out at Bruno's Pub, where he met Mark and a few other colleagues for a drink and to shoot the bull. Today Grey just wanted to be left alone. While Mark appeared tanned and too energetic, Grey felt like he'd been through the wringer over the endlessly long, lonely weekend. Even work, which had always been his refuge, hadn't distracted him from thoughts of Mariah, her short skirts and sassy hair and the guy she was supposedly dating.

Mark grinned and signaled the bartender. "Hey, Bruno, I'll take a Bud and a bowl of your warmed peanuts." He glanced at Grey. "Uh-oh. Straight scotch?"

The only time he drank straight scotch was when he was in a rotten mood. The liquor hit him hard and fast, obliterating all thought and reason. Maybe, if he was lucky, he'd get so inebriated he wouldn't dream of Mariah tonight.

Bruno delivered Mark's beer and the peanuts.

Mark thanked him and gestured to Grey. "Better give this poor man a refill, Bruno."

Grey rattled the ice cubes in his empty glass. "Make it a double."

Bruno lifted a dark, bushy brow but said nothing as he grabbed the bottle of scotch and put a double shot into Grey's glass.

"Looks like I'm gonna be the designated driver tonight," Mark said, snatching Grey's car keys from the bar top and putting them out of his reach. "But I suppose the favor is long overdue, considering how many times you've bailed me out of this place at closing time."

"Yeah, well, if I start singing or something, knuckle me alongside the head, will you?"

"Will do." Saluting him with his beer bottle, Mark took a drink.

Grey reached for a peanut and cracked open the shell, then tossed the warm morsel into his mouth. He and Mark had met at the University of Southern California during their junior year in college. Their similar interests and wild life-styles—that had included partying and lots of women—had bonded them on a masculine level. They'd become fast friends and had remained close over the years. Grey had seen Mark through one marriage and an ensuing nasty divorce with his two little boys caught in the middle.

In Grey's opinion, Mark's crumbled marriage was another prime example of how overrated wedding nuptials really were. Statistics and his own experience with his parents proved that wedded bliss rarely existed. He plowed his fingers through his hair. Why couldn't Mariah understand that?

Mark whistled low and gave Grey a friendly slap on the back. "Man, you got it bad for her, don't you?"

Grey's reply was distinctly profane.

Mark chuckled, unoffended. "Yes, indeed, my friend, you're as good as gone."

Grey didn't care for the sound of that. He'd always been able to walk away from other relationships unscathed, so why couldn't he shake Mariah? Thing was, he didn't want to forget her.

"It's hell getting dumped, isn't it?"

Maybe that's what was wrong, Grey thought, staring at the tawny liquid swirling in his glass. In all his dating years, going all the way back to high school, no one had ever dumped him. He'd always been the one to walk away from relationships before they got too intense, breaking more hearts and enduring the wrath of more women than he cared to recall.

No one had ever walked away from him.

He frowned. Although Mariah's rejection stung his pride and bruised his ego, there was a deeper level to his depression he didn't understand. Without her his life just wasn't the same. And when he rambled around that huge, empty house of his, he'd find himself listening for her voice or her sweet, lilting laughter. But there was no trace of her anywhere. No cosmetics cluttering his bathroom, no scent of her in his bed, no French vanilla coffee in the kitchen cupboard and no butter pecan ice cream in the freezer.

When had those things started to matter?

"Man, have you seen her lately, Grey?" Mark was saying as he scooped up a handful of peanuts and began shelling them. "She's got this great new haircut, and she's traded in her suits for these short little skirts and tight pants. She's got a great...uh, pair of legs."

Grey glared. *They're mine.*

As if reading his friend's thoughts and realizing how

far he'd gone, Mark held up his hands, palms out. "Hey, I wasn't the only one looking, Grey."

"Where have you seen Mariah?" Where in the hell had she gone in her short skirts and tight pants?

"I've seen her a couple of times at Roxy's Nightclub." Mark shrugged. "She was there Saturday night."

"Roxy's?" His stomach felt as though someone had just put it through the spin cycle. "That place is a meat market."

Mark grinned wolfishly. "Yeah, grade-A quality."

Grey gulped the last of his scotch, and the liquor went down like a blazing inferno. "Who was Mariah with?"

"Jade."

"Figures," he muttered. "Anyone else?"

"Just the eight or ten guys who were trying to hit on her." Mark took another swig of beer. "I have to tell you, Grey, she looked hot."

Great. Just what he wanted to hear. "Did she dance with anyone?" And why was he torturing himself with all these questions when he really didn't want to know the answers?

"No, but not for a lack of being asked."

Gray scrubbed a hand over his jaw and swore.

"I went up to her and said hi, and we talked for a while until some guy she knew arrived."

Grey hung his head. "Must've been the guy she said she was dating."

"From what Jade told me, he's a lawyer."

"Did she dance with him?" *Tell me no, because I can't stand the thought of her body being pressed against another man's.*

"No," Mark said.

Grey closed his eyes and blew out a relieved breath.

"But she did leave with him."

Groaning at the intimate images that bit of news provoked, Grey patted his pockets for his Tums and filched two of the chalky tablets. They didn't mix well with the liquor in his belly.

"I've never seen you so torn up over a woman before." Mark's voice was concerned.

Mariah wasn't just any woman. She was, well, everything he'd ever wanted, but hadn't known he needed until she was gone. And he did *need* her, in ways he'd never experienced, and in ways he didn't understand. "Yeah, well, there's a first time for everything."

"Well, get over it." Mark nudged him good-naturedly. "There are other fish in that great big sea of women out there, or at least that's what you told me after Sheila and I divorced." He leaned closer. "That brunette sitting all alone in that corner over there is eyeing you. I'd bet if you gave her the slightest indication you're interested she'd be on her way over."

Grey glanced at the woman in question. She was a looker, with a voluptuous body squeezed into a tight, short denim dress. Long legs, blatantly sexy and wavy hair as long as Mariah's had been. He waited for a tug of sexual attraction. Not even a glimmer of appeal, and it had nothing to do with the liquor he'd consumed, but everything to do with wanting only one woman.

Man, he *did* have it bad for her.

"I'm not interested. She's all yours." Dismissing the other woman, Grey poked at an ice cube, trying to wade his way through his fuzzy thoughts. "I just don't understand what went wrong with me and Mariah. It was good between us. Nearly perfect." He shook his head.

"The spark must be gone."

Grey cast him a narrowed-eyed glance. "The spark?"

"Yeah, you know how women like that spark of excite-

ment they feel when you first start dating. It must be gone for the two of you."

Grey thought the best he could on that one. Sparks between him and Mariah had never been a problem. He could just look at her a certain way and generate enough excitement to keep them on edge until they were alone. "I don't think that's it."

"Sure it is," Mark said confidently. "Trust me on this one."

Abrupt laughter escaped Grey. "Why should I trust you when your relationships fizzle faster than a sparkler on the Fourth of July?"

"But it's good while it lasts," Mark said, laughing. "I'll bet you guys settled into a nice, comfortable routine, right?"

He'd been real comfortable with Mariah. More than anyone in his entire life. She'd been his lover and his best friend. That's why he'd wanted her to move in with him. "Yeah, I guess so."

"That's usually a sign that the romance is gone from the relationship," Mark said, swiping condensation from his beer bottle. "And when the romance is gone, a woman starts looking for deeper stuff. Usually a ring or a forever kind of commitment. That's usually the time to cut loose and bail or reevaluate the relationship."

He didn't want to cut her loose, so maybe he needed to reevaluate what they'd shared. He'd never considered himself romantic. He was a down-to-earth, no-frills kind of guy. And Mariah had never been one for flowers and candy. Then again, he'd never spontaneously, just-for-the-heck-of-it, given her those things.

Maybe she was feeling as though he didn't appreciate her. The thought made him frown.

"Okay, Mark, I've reevaluated the relationship and I

want to keep it." He couldn't believe he was actually soliciting Mark's opinion and advice. "What do I do now?"

"Romance her. Women love that kind of stuff."

Grey cringed at the sound of that. He'd never had to woo a woman in his entire life. He didn't even know how. "I don't know—"

"Trust me, Nichols," Mark drawled. "It's not any different than trying to sway a potential client."

Grey was lost by the analogy. "Care to elaborate on that?"

"It's simple. Invest some money into her—wining, dining, flowers. Jewelry is a nice touch, too. A few romantic gestures, and she'll come around."

Grey's head began to pound. He was awkward with this whole romance angle, but maybe that's what Mariah needed. A little spice and sizzle. He'd tried begging and groveling and that hadn't worked.

He had nothing left to lose.

"THE FLOWERS HAVE GOT to stop." Jade walked into Mariah's office carrying another gorgeous arrangement—this one bright pink tulips. Moving over a bouquet of peach-hued lilies sitting on Mariah's credenza, Jade set the elegant, cut-crystal vase in the cleared spot. "The place is starting to look like a funeral home. But then I guess it matches the mood around here for the past week." She lowered her voice. "You'd think someone died."

Only Jade would say something so morbid. Making a face her sister couldn't see, Mariah set aside a pending invoice for wooden shutters and whirled her chair around to Jade. Surrounding them were at least twenty different bouquets and floral arrangements of all shapes and vari-

ety. In her entire lifetime she'd never received so many flowers.

"How am I supposed to make him stop?" she asked, absently fingering the satiny soft petal of a nearby rose. "Besides, I like having them around. I feel like I've lost my best friend. Grey *was* my best friend."

Jade rolled her eyes. "Grey's merely a man, Mariah. Dogs make better best friends than men do. Dogs are more reliable, trustworthy and they know how to form a real bond." Her bangle bracelets jingled as she fluffed the fat bow around the stemmed tulips.

Mariah sighed, not sure whether she should be flattered or annoyed by Grey's romantic gesture. "I've tried stopping the deliveries, but the florist doesn't want to turn away the business, and the delivery boy informed me of the astronomical amount he's being paid to make sure the flowers reach my office."

Jade raised an inquisitive brow. "Have you tried calling Grey to put a stop to the deliveries?"

Mariah inhaled the floral fragrance floating in the room. The scent was dizzying, and deliciously intoxicating. "Yes, but he hasn't been in his office, and Jeanie doesn't know anything about the flowers."

"I'm impressed," Jade said generously. "At least Grey's not making Jeanie order the arrangements, like most bosses make their secretaries do for their wives and girl-friends."

Mariah agreed, secretly pleased that he was taking time from his busy schedule to contact the florist personally. "I told Jeanie to leave him a note to please stop with the flowers. I guess he hasn't gotten the message yet."

"Or he's ignoring it, which is probably the case." Jade winked an emerald green eye at her, which matched her

bright and splashy summer outfit. "Men don't like to be turned down or dumped."

"I didn't dump him." She hated the way that sounded. "I just thought it best if we go our separate ways."

"It's the same thing, Riah." Jade plucked the little white envelope nestled within the tulips. "Let's see what lover boy has to say this time."

Mariah snatched the envelope from her sister's grasp. With every arrangement that had been delivered Grey had attached a note. The written contents ranged from sweet and romantic, to steamy and erotic, to silly and humorous. Each envelope was a special treat because she didn't know what to expect.

The anticipation of wondering what this envelope contained made her feel giddy. "In case you didn't notice, that's *my* name on the envelope." Giving Jade a tight smile, she tore open the flap and withdrew a florist card with a border of fancy hearts and flowers and Grey's bold writing in the center.

Jade leaned over her chair and read the inscription out loud. "Tu-lips are better than one. Always yours, Grey." She chuckled and shook her head. "The man has a way with words."

Always yours, not *love*, she thought with a heart-wrenching pang. Tucking the card back in its envelope, she put it in her desk drawer with the other cards Grey had sent.

Jade moved to the front of Mariah's desk. "I have to admit, all this is kinda romantic."

"Flowers don't change the way I feel about our relationship."

"No, but it's flattering to know someone wants you bad enough to go to this extreme." Jade dipped her nose into an arrangement of cream-colored roses and inhaled

deeply. "I have to tell you, sis, I didn't think Grey had it in him to be so romantic."

Mariah caught herself when she would have defended Grey. In his own way he'd been romantic, but never mushy or sappy in his pursuit. His approach was always straightforward, earthy and sensual, cutting through any frivolous preliminaries to get what he wanted. Truthfully, that had excited her more than any flowery words or token gifts ever would have.

"Is Richard romantic?" Jade asked, pulling Mariah from her thoughts.

Mariah glanced at Jade, who stood next to her chair, and tried to find an apt but polite description for the man she was dating. "Richard is...nice."

"Nice?" Jade looked at her as if she'd fallen off her rocker. "Tropical fish are nice, Riah. Cupcakes are nice. Richard is a gorgeous male specimen."

And Mariah had begun to notice that he acted like he knew it, too.

Jade perched herself on Mariah's desk and crossed her legs. "Is he a good kisser?"

"He's okay." Richard kissed like he was in a hurry to move on, leaving her little time to catch her breath or protest his groping hands.

Jade leaned closer, eyes sparkling mischievously. "Have you guys, well, you know?"

The thought of doing you-know-what with Richard left her unmoved, although he seemed intent on reaching that goal. She didn't know how long she could hold him off without coming outright and bruising that ego of his. "No."

"No?" Her sister sounded disappointed and a little worried. "He's not gay, is he?"

"He's perfectly straight, and he's got more hands at the

end of a date than an octopus has tentacles." She sighed and rubbed her temple. "I'm not ready for an intimate relationship with someone new yet, and I don't think it's going to work with Richard."

"Well, could you wait until the end of next week to tell *him* that?" She clasped her hands together and gave Mariah a look of sheer desperation. "*Please?*"

Her sister didn't beg often. "Why?"

"Because by then we'll be paid in full for the interior work on his offices."

Mariah understood, though she didn't like playing Richard that way. "Fine. We're going to Dad's birthday party together, but I'm ending things after that. I don't want to string him along."

A voice cleared in the direction of Mariah's office door, and both women swiveled their heads in that direction. A young, petite woman with auburn hair dressed in an elegant silk pantsuit stood in the threshold holding a small, femininely wrapped box with a lace bow tied around it.

"Excuse me," she said, stepping more fully into the room. "Is there a Mariah Stevens here?"

Mariah sat up straighter. "Uh, that's me."

"This is for you." The other woman's smile was dazzling as she handed Mariah the gift from across her desk. "We don't normally deliver our merchandise, but your boyfriend wanted this to be a surprise, and he wanted to be sure you received it."

"Not to mention he probably paid you five times what it would have cost to pay for a courier," Jade mumbled under her breath.

Mariah discreetly pinched her sister's calf. Jade yelped and scooted out of reach. Luckily the other woman hadn't heard Jade's comment.

"Thank you very much for bringing it by," Mariah said graciously.

"It was my pleasure." The woman's eyes sparkled. "Enjoy your gift. Your boyfriend selected it himself."

"Where's it from?" Jade asked once the woman left the office.

Mariah read the gold foil sticker on the corner of the package. "P.J.'s Lingerie and Things."

"Sounds interesting. Hurry up and open it," Jade said anxiously.

Mariah hesitated, not sure if this gift was something she wanted to share with Jade. But her sister didn't look as though she was going to budge until she saw what was in the box.

Before she lost the nerve she untied the lacy bow and ripped off the paper. She pulled off the lid and separated the paisley print tissue surrounding the contents.

Mariah stared, stunned.

"Oh my God!" Jade gasped, a huge grin spreading across her face. "The man certainly knows his stuff!"

The "stuff" Grey had selected consisted of a black satin and lace garter belt, three pairs of black, sexy, sheer-as-a-sigh panties and three sets of sheer black, thigh-high silk stockings with a delicate band of lace encircling the tops. One pair had a black seam running down the center back, another pair had a smoky hue and the last pair had a delicate butterfly embroidered into the stocking on the outside left ankle. Two tiny rhinestones winked at the ends of its antennae.

Swallowing the thick knot in her throat, Mariah retrieved the full-size envelope nestled within the folds of satin, silk and lace. While her sister oohed and ahhed over the lingerie and complimented Grey's taste, Mariah

leaned back in her chair, slid open the envelope and read Grey's message inside the enclosed floral embossed card.

You seem to have taken a liking to pretty lingerie. Let me tell you a fantasy of mine, of you wearing black garters and stockings and a wispy pair of panties beneath a sexy, short dress. It's night, and although there are people around, no one can see us in our private corner as I caress the smooth skin of your thighs where the stockings end, and touch you where you're soft, warm and sensitive.

Remember the fantasy...

Always yours,
Grey

Mariah groaned, her face heating as Grey's provocative words stimulated her feminine senses, leaving her in a frustrated state of desire. He knew how to get her where she was weakest. He had no mercy.

"That good, huh?" Jade asked, a half grin on her face.

Mariah nodded, pressing her thighs together to ease the ache between.

Jade tried to peek at the card, but Mariah quickly stuffed it back in its envelope. Jade pouted. "You're not gonna share, are you?"

Mariah shook her head, still unable to speak. She cleared her throat and reclaimed her box of lingerie, trying her best to put Grey's erotic fantasy from her mind. "What am I going to do with this stuff and all these flowers?" she asked for a lack of something better to say.

"Enjoy it while it lasts," Jade said, sliding off the desk and sashaying toward the door, "because it never lasts for long."

GREY RECOGNIZED the hungry gleam in Mariah's date's eyes, a predatory look that told the male population around him that he was going to get lucky tonight with the woman on his arm. If they hadn't already slept together—and Grey didn't think they had by the stiff way Mariah stood next to the tall blonde—then Mr. *GQ* planned on it happening that evening.

Not if I can prevent it, Grey thought, tamping the savage urge to plant his fist into the lawyer's face. Jim Stevens's fancy black-tie birthday bash was hardly the place to stake his claim on Mariah.

Tugging on the black bow tie around his neck, he watched the pair from across the crowded ballroom at the Hilton. They stood in the reception line to greet Mariah's father, and her mother, Donna. Laughter and conversation, along with dinner music, filtered throughout the room. White-jacketed waiters served appetizers and champagne from sterling silver trays. Men stood in groups talking, while the women in all their finery and glittering jewels moved about the room, some greeting friends and some blatantly checking out the male species.

He should be mingling, saying hello to acquaintances and colleagues and using the gathering to mix business and pleasure. He always managed to drum up potential clients for his security company at parties.

Unfortunately, socializing required ignoring Mariah and the blonde hovering beside her, and he found he couldn't take his eyes off her, or more specifically, her exquisite dress. Body-skimming black lace, lined for opacity but giving the first impression that the dress was see-through, hugged her curves from breast to midthigh. Short sleeves fell off the shoulder, enhancing the swell of her breasts and the scalloped hem of the dress gave way to long legs encased in sheer black stockings and four-

inch heels. Grey stared hard at those stockings, but at this distance he couldn't tell if they were one of the pair he'd bought her. He planned to find out. Soon.

Mr. *GQ* bent his head next to Mariah and said something that made her tilt her head back and smile. Her silky hair swirled around her shoulders and settled like a soft cloud around her face. Mr. *GQ* pressed his hand to Mariah's spine and guided her three steps ahead in her father's reception line.

Grey's gut clenched at that intimate touch, and he thrust his fisted hands into his pants pockets.

"She does look stunning, don't you think?"

Grey glanced at the woman standing beside him, wearing a black velvet sheath that displayed her ample charms. He met cobalt blue eyes brimming with amusement, and scowled. "You're corrupting her, Jade."

Jade laughed, the sound throaty enough to draw the attention of a few nearby males. "And it's so much fun. My straitlaced sister has hatched from her cocoon."

He grunted a reply. Translated, it would have burned her ears.

She stopped a passing waiter and retrieved a glass of champagne. Taking a sip, she regarded him speculatively over the crystal rim. "You mean to tell me, honestly, that you don't like her new look?"

Admittedly, Mariah's new look was starting to grow on him. And just thinking of the possibility of her wearing the lingerie he'd sent her beneath that dress was enough to stiffen certain parts of his anatomy. "I liked her fine the way she *was*, before you decided to play fairy godmother."

Jade grinned as if he'd complimented her. "She needed a change, especially if she expects to catch herself a husband."

Grey looked around for a waiter. He needed a drink. "I'm surprised you don't have a list of bachelors lined up for her," he commented dryly.

She waved her near-empty champagne glass toward her sister. "I thought Richard was a decent catch, but Mariah's being difficult."

His jaw dropped, though he told himself he shouldn't have been surprised. "You set her up?"

She shrugged and drank the last of her champagne.

"Jade, I'm gonna strangle you."

"Naw," she said, batting her lashes at him. "You like me too much."

Despite Jade's brash ways and smart mouth, he did like her. What she needed, he decided, was a man to soften her up a bit.

Jade placed a hand on his jacketed arm, her expression suddenly sincere. "Grey, Mariah's crazy about you, I won't lie about that, but if you aren't going to marry her, you need to let her go."

He couldn't, even though he knew Jade was right. The thought of never seeing Mariah again was tantamount to carving his heart out of his chest.

"I think I'll go meet her new beau." Flashing Jade a smile, Grey strode confidently toward Mariah.

"Men," Grey heard Jade mutter behind him.

Mariah turned, and her gaze fell on him as he approached. She looked startled, torn and a little wary.

The reception line had ended, and the guests around Jim and Donna were breaking up to find their seats for dinner. He'd almost reached Mariah when Jim saw him. Grey couldn't very well ignore the guest of honor.

Grey shook the older man's hand while watching out of the corner of his eye as Mr. GQ led Mariah in the opposite

direction. Something at her ankle sparkled, rhinestones, and Grey knew a moment of supreme satisfaction.

He'd catch up to her later.

Dinner was announced, and Grey found himself seated next to a young woman with short black hair wearing a dress cut lower than legally should have been deemed decent. She had come on to him the moment he'd sat down, making it very clear she was single, available and very interested in him, despite his subtle hints that he was not. Her foot was continually getting tangled around his, and at one point she'd even pressed her hand high on his thigh and squeezed meaningfully, causing him to choke on his chicken.

As soon as the dessert plates were cleared, Grey politely excused himself, ignoring the woman's disappointed pout. It was time to find Mariah before she left the party with Mr. *GQ*.

He strolled around for about ten minutes, searching the mingling crowd for a blonde in an eye-catching dress and thigh-high stockings he'd bought specifically for her. That she'd worn them gave him hope.

Dining music was replaced with something more lively and upbeat for dancing. The parquet dance floor filled up fast, and the chandeliers were dimmed in lieu of flashing strobes. Finally, he spotted Mariah and her date standing in a darkened area of the ballroom. A large potted palm with twinkling lights gave them a modicum of privacy, and Mr. *GQ* was taking advantage of it. The other man was stroking her cheek with his fingers and subtly easing her deeper into the shadows, his head dipping toward hers.

He strode toward them determinedly, his skin heating with jealousy. *Cool it, Nichols. As much as you'd like to*

tighten that bow around Mr. GQ's neck, Mariah wouldn't appreciate the scene.

"Mariah?" Grey said as he neared, causing her date to stiffen and pull away when he would have planted one on Mariah's lips. "I thought that was you!"

Mariah looked at first startled, then relieved by his interruption. She moved out of the shadows and into the open.

The blond man turned and narrowed his gaze on Grey, obviously irritated by his timely intrusion.

Grey ignored him and gave Mariah a wide grin. "It's great to see you, Mariah. It seems like forever, doesn't it? I see P.J.'s delivery made it to you just fine," he added casually, noting that the private exchange was lost on Mr. GQ.

Her gaze widened in shock and mortification, but she managed to recover her composure quickly. "I, uh, yes, I received it just fine. Thank you."

"It was all my pleasure." *Literally.* He turned to the blonde and thrust out his hand congenially. "I don't believe we've met before. I'm Grey Nichols, a good friend of Mariah's."

"Richard Sawyer. Nice to meet you." Reluctantly he shook Grey's offered hand. Both of their grips were strong, with an undercurrent of silent rivalry. "Any friend of Mariah's is a friend of mine."

Sap, Grey thought, wondering what Mariah saw in the other man. A marriage proposal? He shuddered at the thought.

"You wouldn't mind if I stole Mariah for a few moments for a quick dance, do you?" Grey asked pleasantly, making it difficult for the other man to refuse without making him look like a jealous lover. "To catch up on old times?"

A tight smile claimed Richard's lips. "I suppose I could let her out of my sight for one *short* dance."

Don't count on it, buddy. "I'll bring her back just the way you gave her to me."

Grey led a silent and obviously fuming Mariah to the crowded dance floor. A slow song played and he pulled her unyielding body into his arms, relishing the feel of her soft, lush curves pressed against him and the heady scent of her perfume.

She wouldn't look at him, and he noted the tight, angry line of her jaw. "You didn't think you were going to get away with not dancing with me, did you?" He tried to inject a teasing note into his voice.

She met his gaze, her blue eyes glacial. "In case you didn't notice, I'm here with someone else."

Instinctively he tightened his arm around her waist. "Oh, I noticed all right." Disdain coated his words.

"But that didn't stop you from pulling that macho act with Richard."

He didn't think she'd appreciate him reminding her of the relief on her face when he'd interrupted their little interlude.

As they continued to sway to the music, the tension gradually drained from her body, allowing her to lean more naturally into Grey. "I came to this party with Richard. I shouldn't be dancing with other men." She sounded as though she were trying to convince herself of that fact.

"Mr. GQ doesn't seem to be too lonely without you." He glanced to the right, and Mariah's gaze followed his. The aggressive woman who'd been Grey's dinner companion was now busy working on Richard, who didn't seem to mind the obvious passes the voluptuous woman was making.

"I can hardly blame him, after what you just pulled,"

Mariah said, shifting her gaze back to Grey's. Confusing emotions brightened her eyes. "When did you become so callous?"

"I'm a desperate man," he said softly, truthfully. "When did your taste in men take a drastic turn for the worse?"

She bristled and tried to put some distance between their bodies but he refused to loosen his hold. "Who I date is no longer any of your concern."

"Is Richard marriage material?"

Hurt flashed in her eyes, cutting him deeper than he thought possible. "More so than you'll ever be."

He deserved that, he thought, but he didn't like it. The melody ended and segued into a fast song. When Mariah pushed slightly at his shoulders, he let her slip from his grasp and watched her walk away, spine straight and head held high. His gaze dropped to the way her dress outlined her bottom, and a surge of heat flared deep in his belly. Any sane man would cut his losses and move on. His sanity had fled the night she'd gathered up her clothes and left him.

Mariah moved through the throng of guests and made her way out the double French doors leading to a wide veranda that overlooked a garden and elaborate fountain. Finding a secluded, shadowed spot away from the other couples enjoying the sultry evening, she leaned against the cool metal railing and drew a deep breath.

She couldn't stop trembling and it was all Grey's fault. She was furious with him for his behavior. And disturbed that he still had the ability to arouse her so quickly and easily. Dragging her fingers through her hair, she tried to dismiss the way her body still throbbed from the pure torture of being pressed against Grey's.

"So, have you and the lawyer slept together?"

She jumped at the deep voice behind her, not surprised that Grey had sought her out. The man didn't handle rejection well and had the tenacity of a pit bull. "That's none of your business," she said, not bothering to turn around.

His hands curled around the railing on either side of her. The length of him brushed her spine, bottom and thighs. Her heart rate accelerated and a honeyed warmth flowed through her veins. She resisted the impulse to lean back into his heat.

His head lowered to her ear, and the fine hairs at the nape of her neck tingled. Her breath hitched in her throat.

"My guess is that you haven't, but not for a lack of Mr. GQ wanting to." His voice was a low, husky murmur.

Mariah swallowed hard, astonished by Grey's perception. Their clandestine setting and his nearness excited her, and she valiantly searched for the fortitude to stop this craziness.

"I'd bet a hundred bucks he's gonna make his move tonight when he takes you home."

She turned around, a smart retort on her lips—which instantly died the moment she met his gaze. His gold-brown eyes glittered in the moonlight—seductive, hot and wild.

She shivered. She knew that look. Intimately.

The slow, lazy sweep of his gaze took in her hair, her parted lips and the swells of her breasts rising from the bodice of her dress, then back to her face. A wicked smile stretched his mouth. "By the way, you look great tonight."

A melting sensation rippled the length of her. "Grey, you have to stop this," she whispered. *Because I don't have the strength to resist you.*

"I can't." He swore and, grasping her arms, backed her into a dark, private corner of the veranda behind a leafy,

potted ficus tree. Faster than she could gather her wits, his legs bracketed hers and a hand slid from her knee, up her thigh and beneath the hem of her dress.

She gasped in shock, but couldn't move away. "Grey, what are you doing?"

But it was shamelessly obvious what he was doing. His fingers touched the elastic band of her stockings and followed a satin strap to the garter belt she'd donned. The one he'd bought for her.

His grin was pure, unadulterated sin as he whispered, "Remember the fantasy..."

4

REMEMBER THE FANTASY...

Mariah groaned as the words Grey had written flooded her mind, making her remember vividly the things he'd wanted to do to her while she wore the ensemble he'd sent. A part of her brain mocked her for wearing the lingerie when she knew he'd expected her to. On a deep, feminine level she found this whole interlude thrilling.

The voices around the corner and the music floating out the French doors dimmed. The world around her receded, until there was only her and Grey in the secluded alcove. She'd only drunk one glass of champagne, but it could have been the whole bottle for how lethargic she suddenly felt.

She struggled to hold on to any shred of cognizance. "Grey—"

"Shh, baby," he whispered, his warm, damp mouth nuzzling her neck. His fingers traced the elastic band of her panties before sliding back down and out the hem of her dress.

She whimpered, unable to believe the wanton, needy sound had come from her.

He said nothing, but then they'd never needed verbal communication when it came to pleasing and pleasuring the other. His hands outlined the flare of her hips and the dip of her waist, hiking her dress up a few inches. Cool air brushed across the exposed flesh between her stockings

and panties. He continued on, skimming his palms around her breasts to grasp the sleeves of her dress. He tugged gently, and the stretchy lace gave way. Her breasts, full and aching and unrestrained by a bra, sprang free.

Watching her, he licked a finger and touched her sensitive nipple. Her breath caught, and before she could cry out his mouth covered hers in a deep, drugging kiss that made her head spin. His tongue sought and tangled with hers while his hands molded and caressed her breasts. With his foot, he nudged her legs apart until she was straddling his thigh and his erection strained between them.

Lord help her, she wanted him, despite where they were and the risk of being caught. Her body buzzed with desire, and a wet warmth settled between her thighs, where his fingers were again, this time slipping beneath the edge of her panties to touch her intimately.

He stroked her, in just the way he knew made her shatter into a thousand pieces. She moaned desperately, and he buffered the passionate sound with a kiss that weakened her knees. The meltdown began in slow degrees, robbing her of all reason. Her main focus became the intense ache he created within her.

Needing to touch him, she slid her hands inside his tuxedo jacket and rubbed against firm muscle and a heat greater than pure fire. His heavy heartbeat matched her own erratic pulse. She wanted him inside her. It would be just a simple matter of unzipping his pants and her wrapping a leg around his waist. Anyone who happened to walk by would only see two people in a lover's embrace, and not know just how intimately they were joined.

The delicious fantasy, combined with the silken glide of his fingers and the sexiest kisses she'd ever tasted unrav-

eled the last of her inhibitions. Her body convulsed in waves of ecstasy, and she moaned into his mouth and clung to him until the incredible pleasure subsided.

Now she knew how the fantasy ended.

Grey slowly broke their kiss and rested her head on his shoulder until she regained a normal breathing pattern. His own breathing was ragged. He stroked her hair and the length of her spine. Murmuring soothing words, he ignored his own need, which pressed insistently against her belly.

With a tenderness that touched her heart, he adjusted the top of her dress over her breasts and smoothed down the hem. Dazed, she let him tend to her. She had little energy left to do it herself. When he straightened and looked into her eyes, his own were blazing hot and filled with a masculine satisfaction.

He rubbed his thumb over her bottom lip, puffy and damp from his ardent kisses. "'Night, sweetheart," he murmured huskily. Thrusting his hands deep into his trouser pockets, he turned and strolled down the stairs at the side of the veranda and disappeared into the night.

She stared in that direction, long after there was no sign of him. Stunned and bereft by the entire episode, she attempted to calm the tremors still quaking deep inside her. On shaky legs she stepped from the shadowed corner and up to the railing, wrapping her fingers tight around the metal rod.

Tears of anger and frustration burned the back of her throat and filled her eyes. "Damn you, Grey," she whispered vehemently.

He'd seduced her deliberately. Like a possession, he'd marked her, branding her as his so no other man would touch her. So she wouldn't want any other man.

If he were still around, she would have slapped him.

You're just as much to blame, her conscience mocked. *You didn't even try to resist him.*

Two hands settled heavily on the flare of her hips, and a distinctly male body crowded her from behind. Abruptly she whirled around, her palm midway to the man's cheek before she realized it was Richard. She immediately jerked back and dropped her hand, horrified at what she'd almost done.

He looked just as surprised. "Hey, it's just me," he said, his fingers tightening on her waist.

"I'm...I'm sorry." Shaking her head, she tried to move away, but his hold was unrelenting. Short of prying his fingers from her, she was trapped in his firm grasp. "You startled me."

"I didn't mean to." Slowly he drew her forward, sexual prowess gleaming in his eyes. "I was wondering where you'd disappeared to."

Panic settled in and she swallowed the thickness gathering in her throat. Grey's ploy had worked. The thought of another man touching her made her want to bolt, not that she'd ever intended for her and Richard to become that intimate.

"Richard—" She sucked in a deep breath of dismay as his hands cupped her breasts and groped her.

"You like that?" he said near her ear, obviously mistaking her shock for pleasure. "How about we take a walk around the garden area and find a spot where we can be alone for a while?"

She grimaced, and her stomach lurched at the suggestion. Very calmly she removed his hands from her breasts. "If you don't mind, I think I'm ready to leave."

"Great," he said enthusiastically, while passing a friendly hand over her bottom. He squeezed her fanny,

and all but undressed her with his gaze. "My place or yours?"

She squirmed out of his reach. "Mine. I've got a horrendous headache and horrible cramps," she said, effectively dousing the lustful look in his gaze.

MARIAH'S LUNGS BURNED and the muscles in her calves and thighs strained with every stride. The last mile home was always the worst. Normally she had Grey by her side, goading her along to keep her from giving up and collapsing, but those days were a thing of the past. She was on her own, with no weekend running partner.

The thought of Grey, or rather her anger toward him, kept her legs pumping and her mind focused. Grey had always claimed jogging was a therapeutic sport, while she'd thought any form of exercise paralleled physical torture. And in the name of love she'd suffered through a couple of weeks of aching muscles, leg cramps, and bouts of hyperventilation to join Grey on his weekend morning excursion. Before long, running together had become a shared outing, a chance for her to spend quality time with him, even though she'd never learned to enjoy the sport quite as much as he did. However, going home and showering together afterward had been the sweetest incentive to join him.

Following the paved walkway through the park across from her condo, she pulled in an even breath and tried to let go of the tension and fury coiled within her. After Grey's outrageous behavior the night before, her own response to him and Richard's obtuse attitude during the drive back to her place, she wanted nothing more than a little peace and tranquillity in her life.

And no men to complicate it.

Her wish wasn't meant to be. The sound of an ap-

proaching jogger slowed by her side. Without looking, she knew who it was, and refused to acknowledge the man responsible for her present black mood and a sleepless night spent cursing his gorgeous head.

Holding tight to her anger she ignored him, which proved a difficult feat considering he kept staring at her and his arm occasionally brushed hers. Her feminine senses had an annoying way of tingling whenever he was near, and she shook the sensation before she did something stupid...such as be nice to him.

Out of the corner of her eye she noticed he wore nylon running shorts and a muscle shirt drenched in sweat, and surmised he'd been out jogging for at least half an hour. While she drew in ragged breaths and measured every foot closer to her condo in terms of the finish line, he glided beside her, looking physically fit and ready to tackle the world. He was whistling, for God's sake!

She looked up at him and glared.

He grinned. "Good morning, sweetheart," he said cheerfully.

Go to hell, Nichols. Clenching her teeth, she lengthened her stride.

His long, muscular legs easily and effortlessly kept him by her side. "Beautiful day, don't cha think?"

It was until you showed up. Taking a quick detour, she jogged up a grassy knoll, leaving him momentarily behind.

Deep laughter rippled along her nerves, then he was beside her again, undaunted by her obvious attempts to elude him. "Can't say I mind being behind every once in a while. The view is quite nice."

He continued to jog beside her and talk to her, heedless of the fact that she wasn't responding. She kept hoping if she ignored him he'd go away.

No such luck. He was in a great mood. They passed an old lady sitting on a bench feeding the pigeons, and Grey winked and wished her a good morning. As they jogged around a man-made lake he picked up a fly-away Frisbee and flicked it back to the little girl who owned it. He was being entirely too nice, and she silently cursed him for making their breakup so difficult. Why couldn't he be a cretin, as she'd learned Richard could be?

Her final date with Richard the previous night had come to a nasty conclusion, with him expecting something a little more than a thank-you for their time together. And when she'd told him she didn't sleep with men she'd only known a few weeks, he'd spouted a few choice words, then had left in a huff.

"You know, I have to say you're getting good, sweetheart," Grey teased. "Usually by now you're passed out on the curbside."

His subtle jibe provoked her. On impulse, she hooked her foot around his ankle and tripped him. He stumbled and fell to the grass with a string of curses.

Grinning and enjoying her small victory, she turned around and jogged backward so she could look at him. In her sweetest voice, she said, "My, Grey, when did you get so clumsy?"

Faster than a lithe panther, he sprang back up. A determined, you're-gonna-pay look glinted in his eyes. Her heart gave a frantic leap of apprehension. Knowing she was in big trouble, she whirled back around and ran as fast as her legs would allow.

She was no match for his speed and agility. He anchored an arm around her waist, throwing her off balance. With a shriek, she twisted and grabbed a handful of Grey's shirt for support. She fell anyway, pulling him down with her. He swore and grappled to cushion her

fall. He managed to cradle her head in his hand so it didn't hit the ground, but he ended up sprawled on top of her, their faces inches apart.

Mariah was instantly aware of his hard body, slick with perspiration against her own sun-warmed skin. His chest crushed her breasts beneath her thin tank top, and his musky scent filled every breath she struggled to take. The heat he created threatened to consume her. She squirmed for freedom.

He cocked a brow and kept her pinned. "Clumsy, eh? And when did you get such a smart mouth?"

His gaze focused on the mouth in question, his eyes darkening. Alarm bells went off in her head. If she didn't do something fast he was going to kiss her, and if his lips so much as touched hers she didn't know whether or not she had the strength to stop him. God, did she have no shame when it came to him?

His dark lashes lowered, along with his parted lips. She turned her head just as his mouth landed on her cheek. Except that didn't deter him. His lips slid along her jaw, nuzzled her neck, while his body arched subtly, intimately into hers.

Biting back a groan of pure need, she wound her fingers through his thick, damp hair, and gently but firmly pulled his head back. "I suggest," she began in a voice more steely than she felt, "that you get off me before I scream my head off and have you arrested for assault."

His mouth curled into a smile. "Did someone wake up on the wrong side of the bed?" he drawled huskily. "Or just in the wrong bed?"

"*Get...off...me.*" Her low, precise tone held warning.

That dark brow remained cocked but he didn't argue. Slowly—oh, so slowly—he slid off her and stood, then offered her a hand.

Furious with him, she slapped away his help. "You have some nerve!" She gave into the urge and walloped him one in the chest. Her fist bounced off honed muscles and he didn't even flinch. "If you so much as touch me again, I won't be responsible for my actions."

Frowning, he rubbed the spot she'd punched. "You're mad at me."

She released a low growl of frustration and stomped away, certain if she remained near him she'd do more bodily damage. "You catch on quick, Nichols!"

He caught up to her but wisely didn't touch her. "What did I do?"

She stopped. She was still breathing hard, from running and Grey's sensual attack. The second one in as many days. "You know damn well what you did!"

He jammed his hands on his lean hips and tipped his head. "You talking about last night?"

"Yes!" *You dolt!*

A little smirk touched his mouth. "Oh, that." His tone was rough and sexy at the same time.

"Yes, 'that,'" she repeated heatedly. She tried not to think about the incredible, erotic fantasy he'd fulfilled and failed miserably. "Not only 'that,' but you walked away!"

He slowly swiped the back of his wrist across his sweaty forehead, his eyes golden and immensely pleased. "Is that what's bothering you? That I walked away afterward?"

"Ooh!" The enraged sound rumbled in her chest. The man's arrogance was showing, and the thing was, he was damn sexy anyway. She clenched her hands into fists at her sides. "You seduced me deliberately!"

His expression shifted, showing her his serious side. "I can't stand the thought of you sleeping with another man."

He sounded and looked so vulnerable she wanted to weep. "It's not up to you to decide who I sleep with, Grey. Not anymore. And you have no right to...to..."

"Make love to you?" he offered. They hadn't consummated the act, but it had been just as intimate, if not more so because of their covert setting.

"Yes!" There weren't many people in the park, but the few that were around turned and stared at them. She gave them a wan smile.

Grey lowered his voice in deference to their audience. "I didn't hear that mouth of yours say no. Not once. And I didn't do half of what I wanted to."

She gasped. She couldn't help herself, because the images his words projected in her mind were shocking. He was so bad! "You didn't give me a chance to say no! You knew exactly what you were doing the day you sent me that package from P.J.'s."

"Ah, P.J.'s," he murmured reflectively. Standing with legs apart, he folded his arms across his chest and stroked his chin with his fingers. His eyes sparkled wickedly. "I quite enjoyed shopping for you there. And you weren't opposed to wearing what I sent." He perused the length of her lazily, visually stripping away her tank top and cotton shorts and leaving her breathless as a result. "As far as I was concerned, the moment I realized you were wearing the stockings I sent, you were mine."

"That is so chauvinistic!"

He shrugged. "It's the truth. I know you better than you think. You might have attended the party with Richard, but your heart and mind were with me all the way. And I don't think I have to remind you how hot your body was...for me."

He played dirty, getting her right where she was most defenseless. Unable to believe they were having this ar-

gument in a public park, she started in the direction of her condo. "You're crazy," she said, shaking her head.

He caught her arm. "Crazy for you, just like you're crazy for me." His gaze pierced her to her soul. "Look me in the eyes and deny it."

She couldn't. Any denial she might have spouted lodged in her throat and her gaze couldn't quite meet his. The fingers around her arms branded her, and when he brushed his thumb across the soft flesh of her inner elbow, she shivered.

He continued on ruthlessly. "You wore that garter belt and those stockings with the butterfly on the ankle because you wanted me to see it, think of you wearing it and drive me wild."

Again, she couldn't deny his claim. A part of her had done just that.

"Well, it worked, Mariah," he said, a hint of challenge in his tone. "You looked damned sexy last night and Richard was looking to score. And I thought of you leaving with him, and him seeing you in the lingerie I sent, *touching you,* and I couldn't stand it. You're mine, Mariah."

"You're being obsessive," she said on a low hiss of breath. "You treated me like a possession last night, and I resent that!"

"I treated you exactly the way you wanted to be treated." She opened her mouth to issue a retort, but he plowed on. "Maybe your mind is saying we're through, but your body feels differently. Last night proved it."

Her body, unfortunately, had been fine-tuned for Grey's touch, no one else's. Overwhelmed by everything, she squeezed her eyes shut and counted to ten, feeling no more relaxed.

Grey let go of her arm and pushed his fingers through

his tousled hair. "I can't believe you're wasting your time with this guy."

She didn't bother telling him she'd broken things off with Richard the night before. "Just like I wasted time with you?"

His mouth stretched into a grim line, and she would have sworn she'd seen a flash of hurt in his eyes. "Is that how you really feel about us?"

No, she thought, her heart aching for everything they'd shared. *I loved every minute we spent together, and I'll treasure it always. But I can't go on like this, without a firm commitment and the promise of stability.*

Swallowing the words and the rush of emotion rising to the surface, she started to walk away.

He blocked her path, his body a formidable obstruction. "Dammit, answer me."

She looked up at him. The sun silhouetted his body and glinted off his dark hair, giving him a dangerous edge that belied the incredible tenderness and confusion etched on his features. This was the Grey only she saw. Sensitive, gentle and infinitely caring. This was the Grey she wanted to spend her life with...except he didn't believe in happily-ever-afters.

"I love you, Grey," she whispered, giving in to the urge to touch his cheek. The dark and rough stubble lining his jaw pricked her fingers, but she welcomed the bristly texture. "How can I love someone so much and think of our time together as a waste? I regret how things ended—"

He caught her wrist and pulled her close enough to press her hand to his chest. "No one says it has to end," he said gruffly.

"I do." Her smile was shaky at best. The heartbeat beneath her palm kicked into a higher drive. "You can't give me what I need. You're not even willing to try."

His jaw hardened, along with his eyes. "What do you want me to do?"

The impossible, she thought. "I want you to love me."

"How can I give you something that doesn't exist for me?" He let go of her hand and rubbed the muscles at the back of his neck. "Hell, Mariah, I don't even know what love is."

That thought saddened her. How could she make him understand something he'd obviously had no experience with? An emotion she'd been surrounded by her entire life and had taken for granted?

She explained it in the most simplistic terms she could. "Love is caring, and sharing, and wanting to be with the other person so much it hurts when you're apart."

"I'm hurting, Mariah, more than I've hurt in my entire life." The truth of that statement reflected in his eyes. "And I care."

They were missing one important element. "But you don't share. You don't share what's deep inside you."

He cringed, silently admitting the truth. "Would it make a difference if I did?"

She had to think carefully about her answer, because she didn't want to lie to him or give him false hopes about them. "I honestly don't know if it would make a difference now, but maybe then I'd understand why you say you don't believe in love, and why the word *marriage* makes you pale."

He offered no explanation, just stared at her, waging some kind of internal battle she didn't understand. He wanted to share, she could see the anguish in his eyes, but he'd closed himself off for so long he didn't know how to express his feelings. And maybe he didn't want to dredge up all the ugliness seemingly attached to those emotions.

She couldn't force any of it out of him, and she couldn't continue on in a one-sided relationship.

This time when she walked away, he didn't stop her.

"ARE YOU ABOUT READY to wrap it up, John?" Mariah stood in the arched entryway leading into Grey's formal dining room. She watched as the hired photographer shot pictures of the room, richly furnished in mahogany, burgundy and green accents and plush cream-colored carpeting that ran throughout the entire house.

"Another half an hour ought to do it," he said, loading a fresh roll of film into his camera. "I still need to finish up in here, and I want a couple of shots of the sunken living room."

"Okay." She backed out of the room to give John the privacy he required while working. She trusted his judgment and choice of shots; he'd always given Casual Elegance his best.

Pausing in the marbled foyer, Mariah glanced at the gold watch on her wrist and noted the time. She wanted to be out of Grey's house by five and hopefully avoid him in the process. It was three-thirty, and by the time John finished the shoot and packed up his paraphernalia, it would probably be about four-thirty. Grey didn't usually leave work any earlier than six, and when she'd picked up the house key from Jeanie that morning, his secretary had told her he'd be in a meeting for most of the afternoon.

She hadn't seen Grey in over a week, since their "jog" together. She'd spoken to him on the phone to set up a day and time to take pictures of his house, and had managed to keep her call short and strictly business, despite his attempts to steer their conversation to more intimate topics.

The flowers and gifts had stopped, mainly because

she'd flat out refused any deliveries. Although Mariah had gone through a few other breakups in her life, she'd never experienced such heartache and sense of loss. She wondered if the pain would ever go away.

Sighing, she wandered into the sunken living room. It boasted a huge circular brick fire pit in the center, surrounded by a casual but very expensive couch and end tables that had cost a small fortune. Floor-to-ceiling windows overlooked a custom-made pool and deck area, and a landscaped backyard with plenty of room for children to run free. Beyond the yard, Grey had a gorgeous view of the ocean. Down the hall at the far end of the house was Grey's office, a spacious room with a fireplace and built-in bookcases covering one wall. The furnishings were dark, the decor a masculine combination of burnished gold and green.

Bored and restless, Mariah climbed the spiral staircase to the second landing, which she'd avoided all afternoon. She knew the size, shape and design of each room, having been in the house numerous times during its building stage, and then to complete the interior decorating and furnishings. For some reason, today she didn't want to face the intimacy of those rooms and the visions she'd had for one bedroom in particular. She'd put so much of her heart and soul into this house because Grey had encouraged her to, and she'd foolishly believed that someday they might share it. Unfortunately she and Grey had two different concepts of sharing: living together versus marriage.

There were only three rooms on the upper level, a master bedroom, a guest bedroom and a workout room. Avoiding Grey's bedroom, she headed left down the hall and peeked into the room at the far end. A weight set, stationary bike and various pieces of workout equipment

dominated the room. An elaborate stereo system had been added, the speakers mounted on the wall in two corners. It was easy to imagine Grey in here, working out before heading to the office in the morning.

Shutting the door on his private gym, she entered the second room and immediately envisioned something different from how it was currently furnished. Instead of a queen-size canopied bed and armoire, she imagined a white-washed crib with a musical mobile and a matching dresser and rocking chair by the window seat. While searching wallpaper samples for this room she'd discovered a whimsical border in soft pastel colors, the design a carousel of plump, adorable zoo animals that would have matched the imagined nursery perfectly. A nursery for her and Grey's children.

A rush of emotion filled her with lost hope. There would be no babies for her and Grey, no days at the park as a family, and no nights in his arms as his lover. That dream had been shattered weeks ago, yet she couldn't let it go, no matter how hard she tried.

She wanted to believe that Grey could love her, that he could cherish her the way her father cherished her mother. That he'd give her babies and love them as much as she would. But he was hurt and scarred by something painful, memories she didn't understand, secrets he refused to share.

"What's the matter? Don't you like the room?"

Mariah visibly jumped and spun around to face the man lounging casually in the doorway, his hands thrust into his khaki slacks. Her gauze skirt floated around her legs, and the bright matching bangles she'd borrowed from Jade jingled on her wrist.

She hadn't expected him home so early. She should

have guessed he'd surprise her this way. "I'd appreciate it if you didn't sneak up on me."

A lopsided smile graced his lips. "I jogged up the steps and cleared my throat and that didn't seem to get your attention. I've been standing here for at least three minutes watching you, waiting for you to snap out of your trance."

"I wasn't in a trance," she said, smoothing a strand of hair away from her cheek. "Just deep in thought."

He looked as though he wanted to laugh, but held his humor in check. "There's a difference?"

She lifted her chin. "Yes."

"Then what had you so deep in thought?"

She couldn't bear to witness how her maternal thoughts would make him shudder. She kept her silly dreams tucked away. "The house looks absolutely gorgeous."

"Thanks to your expertise." He moved into the room and looked around as if seeing it for the first time. Then he looked at her. "You're everywhere, you do know that, don't you?"

She found it difficult to breathe when he was so near, her every breath filled with the warm, earthy scent of him. "What do you mean?"

"Everywhere I look I see you." His intense gaze held hers like twin magnets. "The wallpaper, the couches, the dining set, this canopied bed. We picked everything out together."

He was doing it again, twisting her heart into one big knot of wanting and need. She valiantly fought the feeling. "I presented you with the choices and you made the final decision, Grey."

"Not on everything," he said softly, his voice stroking her senses like a physical caress. "Just my office. All the other rooms I went with your suggestions."

She hadn't known. The thought both pleased and bothered her. "Do you regret it?"

His smile was a little sad. Reaching out, he gently rubbed the back of his knuckles over her silky cheek. "I only regret that you're not here to share it with me."

She took a step back, dislodging his tender touch. "Grey—"

"I've never been so lonely before," he went on, admitting more than she ever thought him capable of. "I come home from work expecting you to greet me with your wonderful smile, but it never happens. I swear I hear your voice, your laughter, that's how badly I want you here. The last months of the house being built, that's all I thought about, you and me here together. I've never thought of another woman being in my life the way I want you in mine."

Grey had never been one for flowery speeches, yet this sweet confession touched her on such a deep level a lump formed in the back of her throat. And on the heels of that came a fresh wave of anger that he would manipulate her already shredded emotions. Dammit, she was tired of tears and tired of hurting!

"And you know what *I* thought about while the house was being built and we were flipping through sample booklets of wallpaper and carpeting?" She didn't give him a chance to respond, but he definitely looked taken aback by her outburst. "I imagined this room as a nursery."

He frowned, the color draining from his face.

"That's right, Grey," she went on relentlessly, though her heart seemed to shrivel at his reaction. "I imagined children running through the house and playing in the backyard. Children with your dark hair and my blue eyes.

I imagined us sitting at the dining room table as a family and helping our kids with their homework."

He stared, jaw tight.

No, he definitely didn't want to hear about her dreams, and she couldn't go on without them. "I guess we both had different perceptions of the future, didn't we?" she whispered, her fury spent.

A low, rough breath left him. "Yeah, I guess so."

"Mariah, I'm packed up." John's voice drifted up the stairs and into the room. "Let's get a move on."

She stepped around Grey, intending to leave. When her skirt brushed his pant leg he gently grasped the thin material and tugged, forcing her to stop. Her gaze met his stormy one, and she damned her body for its instantaneous response, and he hadn't even touched her physically.

"Mariah—"

"I've got to go," she said quickly, pulling her skirt from his loose fist. Reluctantly he uncurled his fingers, looking away as she fled the room.

His blunt curses burned her ears all the way down the spiral staircase.

"YOU'VE GONE OFF the deep end, Nichols," Grey muttered to himself.

Sinking farther into his Jeep Cherokee's leather seat, he continued to stake out the front of Casual Elegance, waiting for Mariah to emerge so he could execute his rash, last-ditch-effort plan. It was Friday evening, and except for Mariah's champagne BMW, which was parked next to his vehicle, the lot was devoid of cars.

He hadn't talked to her all week, not since the night she'd left his house with her photographer. And every night since, he'd lain in bed and replayed their conversa-

tion in his mind, wishing he'd been able to say all the things she wanted to hear. Wishing, too, that he could offer her all the things she yearned for and deserved. Like marriage and children.

Thing was, he couldn't lie to her, and he couldn't make her promises that would never come true. He didn't know how to love, had only learned from his mother how destructive and desperate that emotion could be. And having had only his own father as a role model, he feared he'd make a damned lousy parent.

No, he couldn't give her the commitment that was all too important to her, but he could give her the answers she sought. He owed her that much.

But in order to do that, he needed time alone with her.

Another ten long minutes and she finally stepped out of the front entrance and locked the glass door. She wore a dressy short outfit in a bright fuschia-and-turquoise print that displayed the incredible length and sexy shape of her legs. Purse and briefcase in hand, she turned and headed toward her car. Knowing it was now or never, he slid out of the Jeep and started toward her.

"Grey?" Her steps slowed, and her gaze turned wary. "Is everything okay?"

He probably didn't look okay, he thought. He wore faded jeans, a T-shirt and aviator glasses that concealed his thoughts and emotions. His stride was purposeful.

"You're coming with me." Grasping her elbow, he escorted her to the passenger side of the Jeep and opened the door. "Get in."

She hesitated, then climbed into the beige leather seat. Confusion and concern etched her features. Taking advantage of her bewildered state, he closed her door and jogged around to the driver's side. Sliding in, he turned

on the ignition. Less than a minute later they were on the freeway, heading north.

She looked at him as though he were a few slices short of a full loaf. He was beginning to think he was.

"Grey, are you going to tell me what's going on?"

Moving into the fast lane, he pressed his foot on the accelerator. He glanced at Mariah, a slow smile spreading across his face. "I'm kidnapping you for the weekend."

She had seen the burst beyond...
window a shaman who didn't she had taking them
and make....late who've on by..... and then
without which....
sensation paper.... to have it there
is..... upward corners in most of have

_____ 5 _____

MARIAH'S JAW DROPPED as she stared at Grey. *Kidnapping her?* "You can't be serious."

"I'm very serious," he said, taking his eyes off the road long enough to glance at her. Even though he wore reflective sunglasses, she could feel his intense gaze as strongly as if the lenses were nonexistent. "Have you ever known me to lie?"

Never, but she couldn't fathom why he'd go to this extreme. "*Why* would you want to kidnap me?"

"So we can be alone," he stated simply.

She frowned at his logic. "We're alone now."

He sped up to pass an old Buick poking along in the fast lane. "It's not enough. I want the weekend."

Three days and two nights of Grey's company. There was a time when she would have been thrilled to have him all to herself for forty-eight hours. Now, it would be pure torture. "This is insane, Grey." His crazy antic caused an equal dose of frustration and anger to course through her. "You can't just kidnap me off the street and whisk me away without anyone knowing where I am."

A smug smile lifted the corners of his mouth, matching the arrogance in his voice when he spoke. "If you haven't noticed, I already have."

With effort, she held her rising temper in check. "Take me back to the shop."

"I will," he promised, "on Sunday."

She tried a more rational approach. "Grey, even if I wanted to—" which she didn't, she tried telling herself "—I can't go somewhere with you for the weekend. I have no extra clothes, no makeup or shampoo—"

"I'll buy whatever you need."

She shook her head. "Jade is going to freak if I don't come home tonight. We were supposed to go out this evening."

His body tensed, and she couldn't help but notice the way the muscles in his thighs rippled beneath the soft denim of his jeans. "To Roxy's?" His voice was tight and disapproving.

She swallowed and lifted her gaze back to his face. "It doesn't matter *where*, only that I have other plans and Jade is going to worry if she doesn't hear from me."

"We'll stop in a bit and you can call her," he offered.

"How generous," she muttered, knowing it was futile to argue with Grey once he'd set his mind to something. "Where, exactly, are you taking me?"

"Lake Arrowhead."

Other than that Lake Arrowhead was a quaint city in the mountains, she couldn't imagine why he'd take her there. "What's in Lake Arrowhead?"

"Privacy."

"I don't understand." And she truly didn't. Why would they need privacy when she'd made it abundantly clear over the past couple of weeks that they were no longer a couple? Not that he'd respected her many requests to keep his distance or let her get on with her personal life. "Why are you making this so difficult?"

He cast her a quick glance. "All I want is one weekend alone with you. No one to bother us, no interrupting phone calls." A lopsided grin creased his face. "Hell, I even left my pager and cell phone at home."

"I'm impressed," she said wryly.

"You should be, considering I've never done this for anyone." Sobering, he reached across the distance separating them and rested his hand on her nylon-clad knee. "Please, Mariah?"

Mariah couldn't breathe for the heat his hand generated, and the sparks created by the fingers lightly stroking the sensitive curve of her leg.

"One weekend," he implored, his voice husky.

Gathering her wits before she softened to his will, she lifted his hand and placed it on the console. "Why should I? It won't change anything between us, and I don't want to spend the entire weekend rehashing our *non*relationship."

"No rehashing, I promise."

"If you haven't noticed, any time we're alone lately all we do is argue, fight and dredge up issues that never get resolved."

"Yeah, I've noticed," he said grimly. Taking off his glasses, he set them on the dash and looked at her for as long as was reasonable considering he was navigating the road. Only then did she see the weariness lining his features and the dullness in his eyes. "Mariah, I've been miserable. I was hoping if we spent the weekend alone, without any interruptions, we could work things out."

A huge lump formed in her throat. More than anything she wanted their relationship to work, but their ideals for the future were too vast. She wanted and needed a husband and babies. He wanted the convenience of having her live with him without the total commitment of marriage. Their opposing views seemed cut-and-dried to her, and not something she was willing to negotiate.

"There's nothing to work out," she said quietly.

He stared straight ahead, his jaw tightening. He was si-

lent for so long she wondered if her words had finally given him the jolt of reality he needed to face the truth—that their relationship was over. For good.

His fingers gripped the leather steering wheel until his knuckles turned white. "Do you remember the day at the park when you said I don't share?"

She remembered everything about that day in the park: his teasing, the press of his body against hers when they'd fallen, their heated debate about love and sharing and especially the anguish in his eyes just before she'd walked away. "Yes, I remember."

"Well, you're right about me not sharing certain aspects of my life, especially my past."

She tilted her head and studied his strong profile, wondering why he was admitting all this now. She didn't have to wait long to find out.

"I've closed myself off to certain emotions for so long, I don't know how to share anything personal. But I'm willing to try...with you."

His willingness to finally open up enough to confide in her surprised and pleased her, yet a part of her remained skeptical. She didn't want to be disappointed again when he found old memories too painful or disturbing to share, and ultimately failed to deliver on his promise.

"Really?" she asked cautiously.

He gave a short nod. "Yes. Can you at least give me a chance?"

Repairing their relationship would take so much more than Grey sharing his past; it would require that he share her goals for the future, goals he didn't envision as his own. A crushing pressure filled her chest, and confusion swirled in her mind. "Grey, I'm all tapped out emotionally—"

"Please?" A desperation like none she'd ever seen

flashed in his eyes. Gone was the self-confident, arrogant attitude he always displayed to the rest of the world. "And if it doesn't work out after this weekend, I'll leave you alone for good. I swear it."

Leaning her head back against the seat, she closed her eyes, wishing things weren't so complicated. Dammit, she didn't want to care about Grey's past or the heartache attached to it, but she loved him too much not to. Didn't she owe him this one small favor? If not for them, then at least to give him the chance to purge himself of the bad memories that kept him from giving her his heart.

The light touch of his fingers fluttered along her cheek. She opened her eyes and met his gaze.

"Please?" he whispered.

She melted, her heart softening just for him. Jade would call her weak and foolish for giving in to Grey, but what was one last weekend with him compared to an eternity without him?

"I'll stay...on two conditions," she finally said.

"*Anything.*"

A small smile touched her mouth. "That we spend the time talking and getting to know one another. I want complete openness and honesty between us."

His dark brows pulled together in a frown. "I've always been honest with you."

"Honest, yes, but not open, especially about your family and your past."

He winced slightly. "Yeah, well, family ties aren't a favorite topic of mine."

"Regardless, that's part of the deal."

"Fine," he said. "And the second condition?"

"We don't make love." Because if they did, she knew they'd spend the entire weekend in bed and not get anything resolved or accomplished.

"You drive a hard bargain, sweetheart," he muttered in disgust.

She smothered a grin. "Deal?"

He drew a deep reluctant breath, but when he looked at her there was a glint in his eyes she didn't quite trust. "Deal."

SHE NEVER SAID ANYTHING about touching or kissing in her stipulations for spending the weekend with him. Grey might have agreed not to make love to her, but he sure as heck didn't plan on being on his best gentlemanly behavior. He'd always found foreplay—mental and physical stimulation—to be the most exciting part of sex. He enjoyed bringing Mariah to a slow, escalating peak of want and need with nothing more than sexy words, the slide of his hands on her body and the caress of his mouth in all the places that made her shiver and moan. No, they wouldn't make love in its purest sense but he planned to heighten her awareness of him every chance he got.

Touching his fingers to the base of her spine, and hiding a smile at the subtle catch of her breath, he walked beside her on the cobblestone path leading to the custom-built cabin overlooking Lake Arrowhead. The trees around them were green and lush, the lake beyond a clear blue. The area was peaceful and quiet, a perfect, private retreat.

"Whose place is this?" Mariah asked curiously.

Retrieving the single house key from his front pocket, he slipped it into the lock and opened the door. "It's Mark's."

Hesitantly she stepped into the foyer and looked around. "I didn't know he had a mountain place."

"It was part of his divorce settlement," he explained. "His wife got the Mercedes and the house in Laguna Ni-

guel, and he was awarded this cabin. He still brings his boys up occasionally."

She strolled into the cozy kitchen and set her purse on the dinette table situated in front of a bay window. "It was nice of him to let you use the place."

Mark had been more than happy to hand over the key, along with the suggestion to heat up the spa and take advantage of the romantic atmosphere. Grey intended to do both. "If you'll open up the place, I'll bring in the groceries and other things."

"Okay," she said, moving into the living room and toward the sliding doors that led to a redwood balcony.

Jogging back to the Jeep, Grey opened the rear door and hefted a couple of bags of groceries into his arms. They'd stopped at the market for some basic staples and the necessary toiletries for Mariah. The market's deli special of lasagna and garlic bread was their dinner. When she'd gone to call her sister on a pay phone, he'd slipped into an exclusive boutique a couple of doors down and bought her a few outfits for the weekend, along with some underthings and a pair of leather sandals.

Once the car was unloaded and a cool breeze flowed through the house, Grey warmed their dinner in the oven and they sat at the kitchen table to eat. Outside, dusk moved in, bringing with it the serenade of crickets. He kept the conversation light, establishing an easy, comfortable setting.

Once dinner was finished and the kitchen cleaned, he turned to Mariah, ready to put his plan of seduction into action. "How about a dip in the hot tub outside?" he asked.

She folded a dish towel and placed it on the counter, suspicion filling her eyes. "I thought we were going to use this time together to talk."

He grinned to put her at ease. "No reason why we can't do that while relaxing in the spa."

"I didn't have time to pack a swimsuit," she said sardonically.

"You don't need one." She opened her mouth to protest, and he cut her off. "If it makes you feel any better, I didn't bring one, either."

She crossed her arms over her chest, though a half smile curved her mouth. "This sounds just a little too convenient."

He couldn't deny her claim. The suggestion *was* convenient, one he'd be a fool not to take advantage of. "No funny stuff, I promise." He held his hands out in a show of trust. "We'll even sit across from each other."

Mariah stared at Grey, weighing his sincerity. The man could be so charming and persuasive, she found it difficult to deny him something so casual as sitting and relaxing in a hot tub together. It was the "naked" part she had a problem with. But it was getting dark outside, and they were both adults capable of keeping their desires on a tight rein. At least, she was.

"Well?" he prompted. "Should I go heat up the spa?"

She could do this and be totally unaffected by Grey. She needed to learn that particular discipline, and this was as good a time as any to show herself just how much willpower she possessed. To prove her determination, she lifted her chin and said, "Go ahead. I'll be out in a few minutes."

With a triumphant grin Grey slipped out onto the redwood deck. Seconds later the sound of the spa's jets could be heard as they sputtered and chugged to life.

Grabbing her purse, Mariah enclosed herself in the bathroom and stripped out of her shoes, outfit and underthings. She wrapped a towel around her and tucked the

end securely, covering herself decently from her breasts to just above the knee. Finding a barrette in her purse, she piled her hair on top of her head the best she could. There was nothing she could do for the shorter strands that fell free and wisped around her face and neck.

By the time she returned to the deck, steam curled from the rapidly bubbling water. Grey sat on a redwood chair, bare feet propped on the railing and his hands clasped on his belly as he gazed out at the full moon that had risen above the lake over the past hour. He looked altogether too sexy and tempting and he'd yet to shed his clothing. Awareness unfurled within her, spreading a pleasant tingling along her nerve endings and making the towel around her body feel coarser against her skin than it actually was.

She shifted restlessly on her feet. So much for being unaffected. So much for willpower.

Picking up one of the two glasses of wine on the small round table beside him, he took a deep swallow of the drink, then refilled his glass before glancing at her. "Beautiful night, isn't it?"

All of a sudden she felt like a schoolgirl, which was ridiculous considering how intimate she and Grey had been. Absently double-checking the knot holding the towel in place, she looked up at the twinkling stars in the clear night sky. "Uh, yes, it is."

His warm and lazy gaze did a slow, appreciative perusal, from the haphazard knot of hair on her head to the tips of her bare toes. "You gonna get in or are you gonna stand there all night?" Amusement tinged his voice, but his eyes were all golden heat.

Her stomach fluttered. "I'm, um, not dressed."

Standing, he set their glasses of wine on the rim of the tub, then stripped off his shirt and tossed it on the chair

he'd just vacated. "I won't be either in a second." Unbuckling his leather belt, he unzipped his fly and hooked his fingers into the waistband of his jeans and briefs.

She sucked in a breath, though his boldness shouldn't have surprised her. The man didn't possess an ounce of modesty. "Grey!"

"What?" The look he gave her was a stirring combination of innocence and sin. "It's not like you've never seen me naked." The jeans and briefs whooshed down his legs, and she averted her gaze, though from the corner of her eye she saw a flash of smooth, muscled skin and the toned curve of his buttocks as he stepped into the spa.

"Ahh." He sighed contentedly as he stretched his arms along the rim. "This feels great. Your turn."

She wasn't about to give him a free show. "Close your eyes."

The rogue laughed, the sound deep and throaty. "I thought I'd stripped you of all inhibition long ago."

He had, and she'd be the first to admit that she'd done things with him that had shocked her sensibilities in the beginning. Eventually, though, she'd gained enough confidence to freely explore her sensuality and desires. But that had been before, when she'd believed they had a future together. The uncertainty of their relationship made her more discreet.

"Eyes closed, Nichols."

He grunted a complaint but complied. "For crying out loud, Mariah, I've been intimate with that cute little mole on the inside of your thigh and that bunny-shaped birthmark on the curve of your breast and you're worried about me seeing a glimpse of...oh, man," he groaned as she stepped into the spa, completely naked.

Mariah froze, her gaze darting to his wide-eyed one as he stared at her breasts, the indentation of her waist and

the juncture of her thighs with a hunger that sent her pulse into a tailspin. Quickly, she sat across from him, submersing herself to her shoulders in the hot water.

She glared at him. "You promised not to look!"

He dragged a wet hand over his jaw. "I'd never be so foolish as to promise any such thing. Do you realize how long it's been since I've seen you naked? Since we've made love? *Really* made love?" Need thickened his voice.

Beneath the froth and caress of water her nipples tightened into aching points. She could give him the exact days, narrowed down to the hours and minutes if he really wanted to know. "I have no idea."

"It's been too long," he said. "Much too long, don't you think?"

She gave a one-shoulder shrug. "I haven't thought much about it at all." *Liar*, her body taunted.

He took a drink of wine. "So, is Richard going to wonder where you are this weekend?" The change of subject made his features tighten and turn grim.

She wasn't sure why, but she took pity on him and divulged the truth. "Richard and I aren't dating any longer."

A low, audible sigh of relief escaped him, though his gaze never left her face. "Why not?"

She stretched out her legs and her foot touched his at the bottom of the spa. *Because he's not you. Because you hold my heart and soul. Because I can't forget you, even when I do my best to try.* "It's none of your business."

Grey trapped her foot between his ankles, and before she could rescind the move he reached down and caught her leg and settled her foot on his hard thighs. She gasped and jerked back, but lost the match.

"Relax, sweetheart. I only want to massage your foot."

She should tell him no, but he was already rubbing

those incredible hands and fingers of his along her sole and heel. It felt too wonderful to fight, and as long as he didn't explore above the calf, she'd be okay. She relaxed slightly, trying not to think how close the foot resting in his lap was to his—

"Richard wasn't any good in bed, was he?" Grey asked abruptly.

She choked on incredulous laughter. "We never got that far!"

"Good." His thumbs pressed into her arch, the satisfied gleam in his eyes slowly fading. "Who's next on Jade's list of eligible bachelors?"

"No one." *Thank God.*

"And what about your father's?"

She smiled and sank deeper into the water until her neck rested on the rim. Her earlier tension gradually ebbed from her body. "Don't you think I can find my own dates?"

"Oh, absolutely. I just know your father when it comes to his single, available daughters."

She tilted her head and bravely settled her other foot on his knee for equal treatment, wiggling her toes. "Do you now?"

"Yep." Beneath the eddying water, his finger slowly slid between her toes, caressing the sensitive skin there. She shivered, and a smile lifted his mouth. "Remember how we met?"

How could she forget that monumental moment when she'd looked into his gold-brown eyes for the first time and become a devout believer in love at first sight? "Yes, I remember. We met through a consultation appointment."

"Your father set us up."

"He referred you to Casual Elegance," she corrected. Lifting her glass of wine from the side of the spa, she

drained the rest of the pale liquid. A languid warmth within her mingled with the heat of the spa's jets, making her lazy and lethargic.

"He set us up, Mariah," he said, the skin around his eyes crinkling in humor. "As soon as I mentioned I was building a house he told me his daughter was the best interior designer in southern California. So I let him set up an appointment with you."

She frowned, recalling her father's enthusiasm when he'd called months ago to set her up with a potential client who owned his own security firm. As much as she loved and adored her father, she wouldn't put it past him to do a little matchmaking, just to speed up the process of one of his daughters getting married.

"You didn't have to see me," she said quietly.

"Your father insisted, and since he was about to become a major account for Nichols' Security I figured it couldn't hurt to see his daughter about a consultation." He stroked his hand along her ankle and cupped her calf in his palm before kneading the taut flesh, loosening the muscle. "Though I have to admit I expected to find a spinster."

A tiny groan of pleasure slipped from her. Instinctively she flexed her foot. "And what did you find instead?"

He gazed at her with a tenderness he rarely displayed. "Instead I found the woman of my dreams."

She rolled her eyes to dispel the softening of her heart. "And I thought you were the most arrogant man I'd ever met."

He grinned wolfishly. "I knew what I wanted."

She shook her head at his presumptuousness. "And it wasn't to see carpet samples."

"No, it certainly wasn't that," he agreed. "And we didn't get much business done that night, did we?"

She reflected on that evening, and how he'd deliberately steered their conversation away from business, and onto more personal topics...such as, was she seeing anyone? "Not after you said you just *had* to kiss me, then did just that without my permission."

"I didn't need it. Your eyes said you wanted the kiss as much as I did."

Scooping a handful of frothing water, she trickled it over a dry patch on her shoulder. "You obviously saw what you wanted to."

"You didn't object." He leaned forward, his thigh flexing where her foot rested. "In fact, if I recall correctly, your mouth opened beneath mine for a deeper kiss when I'd only intended to give you a chaste one."

She lifted a brow. Nothing about Grey had ever been chaste. Not the way he'd relentlessly pursued her, not the way he made love to her the first time and every time since and certainly not the way he kissed. She was certain that if she hadn't parted her lips beneath his he would have found a way to coax her into giving him the taste he really wanted.

His thumb pressed into the ball of her foot and rubbed in sensuous circles. "Admit it, sweetheart, you wanted it every bit as much as I did."

"You think too highly of yourself, Nichols."

His gaze narrowed challengingly and dropped to her mouth. "You gonna make me prove how much you want it, and like it?"

Her heart raced. She wouldn't put it past him to make good on his threat. Summoning strength against the desire ribboning within her, she removed her feet from his lap and gave him the confession he sought. "Okay, I'll admit I was attracted to you."

His expression turned cocky. "So much so that when I asked for another appointment you gave me one."

"To talk business!" *Not to be swept off my feet by you.* Which is exactly what he'd intended, and exactly what had happened. "You hired me as a consultant, Grey."

Grinning, he dipped his hands into the water and ran all ten fingers through his hair, dampening the strands away from his face. "It was the only way I could get you to see me. I've never had to work so hard at getting a woman the way I had to work to get you."

His admission secretly pleased her. "It was good for you."

He wiggled his dark brows. "The chase wasn't half as much fun as your surrender."

Perspiration beaded on her upper lip, as much from the steam rising off the water as the hot look in Grey's eyes. The man was a master in seduction, wearing down her resistance with kisses and intimate caresses that shattered all coherent thought, until she surrendered heart, body and soul. "You didn't play fair."

"I was crazy about you," he said softly, meaningfully. "I still am."

Her throat closed up with emotion, and she looked away, out into the darkened woods around Mark's cabin. She believed Grey, which made their breakup all the more difficult to handle. But the difference between being crazy about someone and loving someone was too great when it came to making a commitment.

Suddenly tired and weary of trying to sort out her feelings for Grey, she started to stand. But remembering her state of undress, she promptly sat back down. "I, uh, think I need to get out before I shrivel up."

Grey nodded his agreement, knowing they were close to the "rehashing" point. He didn't want to end their re-

laxing evening with an argument. Apparently neither did she.

While she kept her gaze averted, he stepped from the tub and quickly dried off with her towel. Tugging his jeans over his damp skin proved to be a challenge. Once he'd zipped his fly and was decently dressed, he handed her the towel.

"I don't suppose you need help drying off?" he asked.

Her fingers brushed his as she reached for the towel. Desire flared in her gaze, the only sign that his touch and nearness had any affect on her. "I think I can manage on my own, thanks."

He grinned. "Doesn't hurt to ask."

Giving her some privacy, he turned toward the dock railing and listened to her step from the spa. The image of her body glistening with water and moonlight taunted him, and it took an incredible amount of control to keep from turning back around and looking his fill...and taking his fill. Grinding his jaw against the rush of heat pooling low in his belly, he wrapped his fingers around the railing and eased out a tight breath.

"Do you have a shirt I can sleep in?" she asked.

He took that as his cue that he could turn around, and did so. The twisting in his gut increased. She looked like a night nymph...a vision of purity and innocence that grabbed him hard. Her damp hair was loose around her face, and her flushed skin was beaded with drops of water that trickled from her neck to the cleavage swelling above the top of the towel. He wanted to lap the trail with his tongue, taste her skin, her breasts, her belly....

"Grey?"

Jerking his gaze back to her face, he searched his memory for what she'd asked. Oh, yeah, something to sleep in.

"I bought you a nightgown at that boutique I stopped at." Turning off the spa's jets, he pulled the cover over the top.

She fingered the hem of the towel. "Did you buy it for *my* comfort or *your* pleasure?"

He laughed deeply. "Come see for yourself, Ms. Skeptic. I was on my best behavior."

She followed him inside the house and waited while he rummaged through the bags the boutique had given him. Into the fourth package, he finally found what he'd been searching for.

He held up the simple peach chemise for her inspection. "Not a bit of silk or lace, and the hem hits below the knee. Does it meet with your approval?"

Pleasure lit her gaze and she smiled. "You surprise me sometimes, Grey. It's perfect." Taking the gown from him, she sashayed toward the bathroom.

Grey watched her swaying hips the entire way, wondering what she'd say if he told her he'd also bought her a red silk-and-lace number that left little to one's imagination. A smile twitched his mouth. He was saving that scrap of nothing for later, when she finally came to her senses and realized they belonged together.

Digging through the duffel he'd packed for himself, he withdrew a pair of sweatpants and changed while waiting for Mariah. She emerged from the bathroom, her face freshly scrubbed and the scent of mint toothpaste clinging to her.

She placed her bundle of clothing on a nearby chair and tried to hide a yawn behind the back of her hand. "Where am I sleeping?"

"I know where I'd like you to sleep." In his arms, snuggled against him like a warm, content kitten; her breath sighing on his chest; the fragrant, feminine scent of her surrounding him. And in the middle of the night her

hands would roam, stroking over his belly, down his thigh until she found him hard and ready for her. God, he missed the intimacy and closeness of sleeping together, of reaching for Mariah, pulling her beneath him and them coming together in moans of mutual pleasure.

"We wouldn't sleep," she said huskily, reading his mind.

Considering the arousal he hadn't been able to tame since slipping into the spa with her, she was right. "Would that be so bad?"

She ran her hand over the back of the tweed sofa separating them. "We made a deal, Grey, and we haven't even fulfilled the first condition, let alone dealt with the second one."

"We'll talk," he promised in a low, frustrated growl. Stepping around the sofa, he grabbed her hand and led her down the hall to the master bedroom. "We've got two more days to talk about anything and everything."

She dug her heels in at the bedroom door, bringing them both to a sudden halt. "Good night, Grey."

He didn't like being dismissed, not when he knew he was going to spend a sleepless night tossing and turning on the couch while she slept snug and sound in a soft bed. Alone.

Giving in to the urge to do what he'd been dying to do the entire evening, he slid a hand into the hair at the side of her face and guided her two feet back until her spine pressed against the wall. Her lips parted on a gasp and her eyes widened. He lowered his head to steal a kiss. At the last second she turned her face and his lips grazed her jaw. Damn, he should've known she'd do that!

"Grey, no," she said, a wispy catch to her voice.

He chuckled and pulled back, stroking his thumb over her cheek. "Your willpower amazes me."

She looked up at him with stormy blue eyes. "Yeah, me, too. You're hard to resist, Nichols."

His fingers massaged her scalp and tangled through her hair. He missed her long hair, but he was getting used to this shorter sophisticated cut and the way the strands filtered through his fingers like skeins of silk. "Then why are you resisting what we both know you want?"

"Because I've never been one for gratuitous sex." Taking his hand away from her face, she attempted to step around him.

He trapped her with his hands on either side of her head. "Is that what you think it would be? Gratuitous sex? A wham-bam-thank-you-ma'am kind of romp?" He was annoyed that she'd even suggest such a thing.

That stubborn chin of hers lifted. "In some ways, yes. You've always had a healthy sexual drive and I'm sure you're not used to abstinence. That is, if you have been," she added.

His irritation level climbed a notch. "Of course I have been!"

She looked startled by his snappish tone. "I didn't mean that insultingly."

"Well, it sure as hell came across that way," he said gruffly, scowling down at her.

She let out a long sigh and turned her head away, as if it pained her to be this close to him, to look at him. "You're free to date other women, Grey, just like I dated Richard. And what you do with those women is your own business."

Furious with her impersonal tone, he grasped her hand, pulled it between them and pressed her palm against the erection straining the front of his sweats. Her gaze flew to his and a strangled sound hitched in her throat. The shock

value was worth the pure torment of having her hand cup him so perfectly.

He leaned close, brushing his lips across her cheek, her throat, just beneath her ear. "Thanks for your permission, sweetheart. Unfortunately there's only one woman who turns me on." He rocked into her palm, squeezed her fingers along his ridged length and grew impossibly harder, thicker. He closed his eyes and groaned at the sensation of both pain and pleasure. "Only you, Mariah," he rasped. "My reaction to any other woman pales in comparison to how you make me feel."

Her breathing grew shallow, and when he eased up the pressure of her hand, she didn't let him go. Instead, her fingers stroked him rhythmically. "And what do I make you feel, Grey?"

His head fell back and he tried to think with his brain, not that other part of his anatomy ready to explode. What did she make him feel? She made him feel...warm, cherished and needed. No one had ever made him feel those things, not his parents or any other woman he'd ever dated. And he had no idea how to express his emotions without sounding like a sap.

So, instead, he focused on the physical sensations rippling through his body. "I think the answer is obvious."

Disappointment clouded her features, and she pulled her hand away. "Yeah, I guess it is," she said regretfully. "Good night, Grey." She slipped into the bedroom and closed the door. The lock clicked softly, solidly.

He stared in bewilderment at the oak door, unable to believe she actually felt as though she needed to secure herself from him.

Resting his head against the wall, he squeezed his eyes shut, swearing at his own stupidity. "Nothing like taking the subtle approach, Nichols," he muttered in self-disgust.

6

"IT'S ABSOLUTELY HUGE!"

Leaning close to Mariah's side, Grey whispered low in her ear, "Do you want it?"

She gasped, her eyes widening in shock. "It's much too big."

He grinned lazily and stroked a finger over the curve of her shoulder and down her arm. She shivered in response. "You've never had a problem handling 'big' before," he murmured.

His innuendo earned him a not-so-subtle jab in the ribs, but the smile in Mariah's eyes soothed his wounded ego. "We aren't talking about your swelled head or that other 'big' part of your anatomy."

He perfected little-boy innocence. "We're not?"

She tapped a finger against the display window outside a jewelry store in the Arrowhead village, indicating the five-carat diamond ring glittering against black velvet. They'd been strolling along the shop fronts after a light breakfast at a gourmet coffee shop when the extravagant piece of jewelry had caught her eye. "*That* is huge in a way you could never match."

"My family jewels are more impressive than a mere diamond," he said with feigned indignation.

She tilted her head back and laughed—the light, throaty sound warmer than the bright sun overhead. Somewhere between last night's not-so-pleasant parting

and this morning, the tension between them had eased. At least the emotional tension, he thought with a grimace, knowing the physical frustration wouldn't abate until he got Mariah back where he wanted her. In his bed. And in his life.

And he had today and tomorrow to sway her to his way of thinking, to convince her that living together was far more practical than marriage.

She slanted him a look of amusement. "I guess you haven't heard that diamonds are a girl's best friend."

Sweeping a splayed hand up her spine, he slid his fingers beneath her silky, shoulder-length hair. Her nape was warm, and he stroked the soft skin there. "Diamonds might be a girl's best friend, but the family jewels are far more valuable."

She lifted a sassy brow. "How do you figure?"

"They're nice to admire, fun to play with and provide hours of pleasure," he said, enjoying their playful, intimate banter.

Her mouth curled into a private smile. "A gift that keeps on giving, hmm?"

"Absolutely."

He glanced back at the ring, impressed how it caught the light in an array of shimmering colors. Even *he* had to admit that the ring was stunning, in design and size. He'd never given jewelry to any of the women he'd dated before Mariah. That kind of gift seemed too personal and way too intimate. But he wanted to give Mariah this ring she seemed to admire, as a token of his affection for her. A reminder that he cared for her, liked having her in his life and wanted her there for as long as it lasted.

"Do you like it?" he asked casually.

She tilted her head, studying the ring thoughtfully. "It's different. And for as big as it is, it's very elegant."

Pushing his fingers into the front pockets of his navy shorts, he released a breath before saying, "If you want the ring, it's yours." He grimaced at his brusque tone. *Way to go, Nichols. That was a real romantic gesture.*

She gaped at him. "You're serious?"

As serious as he could be about her and their relationship. "Would I joke about something so obviously expensive?"

"It's a bridal set, Grey," she said wryly. "A *wedding* ring."

A wedding ring? He blanched, and his stomach rebelled at the thought. He groped for his Tums before remembering he'd purposely left them at home, determined to survive the weekend without them. He should have known better.

He gave a shrug that belied the tension coiling through him. "A ring is a ring. A trinket with only as much sentimental value as a person puts on it."

She crossed her arms over her chest, looking mildly irritated. "And you obviously don't put much value on this ring."

"Sure I do," he argued, not liking that she was discussing his feelings for her in terms of diamonds and gold. Now he knew why he'd steered away from giving jewelry to the women he'd dated in the past. "This ring would be a token of how much I care for you. A gift that you'd be able to wear and enjoy and that would remind you of me when you looked at it."

She lifted a brow. "Sort of like a souvenir of our time together?"

A souvenir? He bristled, but held his aggravation in check. Why was she making this so difficult when all he'd wanted to do was give her something that would bring her pleasure? Why did there have to be any excess emo-

tional baggage attached to the gift? "Consider the ring a keepsake." He mentally winced. Damn, that didn't sound right, either.

Her mouth thinned in displeasure. "Like something you'd give a mistress."

Frustration flared within him, needling his temper. "I never said you were my mistress."

"I would be if I accepted that ring under any other terms than what it's meant for," she said passionately. "That ring is supposed to bind two people in love, Grey."

"Really?" A burst of cynical laughter escaped him, bringing with it an edge of hostility and defensiveness that made his voice rise. "A ring never made my father love my mother, nor did it bind my mother to any of her subsequent four husbands. And I seriously doubt the newest ring she slipped on her finger is going to keep her eternally devoted to my newest stepfather!"

Long moments passed as they stared at one another. Tourists and locals walked past, but Grey paid them no heed. His jaw clenched hard. God, he hated the mixture of incredulity and shock etched on Mariah's face, but she'd wanted honesty. And he'd only given her a small dose of the unattractive truth about his past.

"Your mother has been married *five* times?" she finally asked, her quiet voice filled with disbelief.

"Yeah," he said roughly, vividly remembering two of those divorces as a youth, and the confusion and resentment that grew with each separation. "And following every breakup, my mother always fell into a deep state of depression, ignoring everything and everyone, including me, to wallow in self-pity until another man came along and gave her the smallest bit of attention. She'd cling, thinking herself in love, wanting that elusive emotion so badly she imagined it even though it wasn't there."

It had been a vicious cycle of men and relationships with his mother, one that Grey had been inevitably thrust into the middle of. And with each new beau of his mother's he'd grown more belligerent and hostile in an effort to hide his pain. His own father hadn't wanted him, had verbally degraded him, and his mother had been so wrapped up in her own search for happiness and acceptance he'd become nothing more than a nuisance, an extra piece of baggage she had to tow along for the ride.

His mouth twisted into a bitter smile. "Quite a track record in the Nichols family, wouldn't you say?"

She gave her head a brisk shake, compassion softening her features. "It's not *your* track record, Grey."

"Exactly." Nor would it ever be, he'd vowed long ago. If he didn't get married he wouldn't have to worry about divorce. And if he never had children, there wouldn't be anyone to suffer from his lack of parenting skills, or from his inability to love.

Disgusted with their topic of conversation and how terse he'd been with Mariah, he turned and walked away, his focus on the clear blue lake beyond all the shop fronts.

Mariah started after him, not about to let him take the easy way out. He couldn't make a statement like that then walk away, leaving her teetering on the edge of something far more profound. As difficult as this might be for him, it helped her to understand his reasons for keeping his heart under lock and key. And possibly give her the ammunition to battle his fears.

She halted his stride with a hand on his arm. "Grey, wait." His body stiffened, and when he finally met her gaze, the misery and emotional turmoil reflected in his eyes yanked at her heart.

"Oh, Grey," she whispered, wishing she had the ability

to chase away the dark shadows eclipsing his eyes. "I'm so sorry."

His frown deepened. "Why should you be sorry?" he asked, his tone gruff. "My mother's failed relationships aren't your fault."

He'd misunderstood. She was sorry for the young boy who'd seen the worst of relationships and marriages. She was sorry that experience had taught the man he'd become to be wary of commitment. And she was so very sorry he thought of marriage as something distasteful, rather than the joyful union she knew it could be. Her own parents and grandparents were proof that love went a long way in a relationship if two people were willing to work at it.

She'd seen the best of marriage. He'd seen the worst. Could she blame him for being so cynical?

"And it's not your fault, either," she said gently. "You aren't responsible for the choices your mother made."

He averted his gaze, but not before she caught a glimpse of vulnerability. "Maybe not, but my mother's short-lived relationships and my father's resentment of his marriage are proof that love, if such a thing even exists, doesn't last."

She sighed in frustration. A light breeze blew off the lake, ruffling his sable hair across his forehead and flirting with the skirt of the summer culotte outfit Grey had bought for her. She waited for a more significant comment from him, but when it was obvious he had no intention of talking further, she decided it was time to make him listen.

Touching her fingers to his jaw, she turned his face back toward her, ignoring the ominous slant of his brows. "Nobody ever said marriage was easy, Grey. My parents had plenty of disagreements, but they communicated and

worked through their problems. That's how you make love last. Marriage is a commitment, a pledge to respect one another and compromise when you both want different things. You can't ignore obvious problems or bail out of the relationship at the first sign of trouble."

"You bailed on me," he hastened to point out.

She couldn't help the smile that pulled at her lips. Only Grey would think of their breakup that way. "That's different. You left me nothing to fight for. If you gave me something, *anything* worth fighting for, I'd be by your side forever."

He cocked a brow. "Something like marriage?"

She was gratified to see that the mention of marriage hadn't caused him to turn pale this time. Hope bloomed within her. "I'd like your love first."

He stared at her for what seemed like an eternity. Then he pulled in a deep breath and opened his mouth to speak, but she stopped his flow of words with a hand pressed gently to his warm lips. She didn't know what he'd been about to say, but she didn't want him to shatter this fragile moment with a denial or excuses. That, and she wasn't finished with him.

"Don't say anything, Grey. Just think about everything I've said, okay?" She didn't wait for a response because she didn't need one. "You know how I feel about you and that hasn't changed in the time we've been apart. But I don't want you to tell me you love me because you think it's something I need to hear. When and if you ever say those words I want it to come from your heart."

Removing her hand from his mouth, he pressed her palm onto his chest. Beneath his beige knit shirt his heart beat at a rapid pace, almost frantically. "What if that never happens?" he asked uncertainly. "Love, that is."

It would, she thought, if only he'd allow himself to

search within his soul for what was already there. An emotion most likely rusty from neglect, but with time and care, his ability to love could be something brand-new and wonderful for him. "If love never happens for you, then I guess we weren't meant to be. And if love does happen, you'll know it without any doubts."

Skepticism shone in his eyes, and his hand tightened over hers. "Dammit, Mariah, I don't want to lose you, and I hate being without you."

She smiled. "That's a real good start to love."

He looked surprised, but not totally adverse to the thought. He drew her closer with a possessive sweep of his hand along her spine. An instantaneous heat flared within her, matching the fire in his eyes.

"I hate it when another man touches you," he growled low and deep in his throat.

She laughed, feeling light inside. "I think that's called jealousy, not love."

"I still hate it," he muttered, his lip puffing out in a boyish pout.

She smoothed a hand along his shirt collar. "You're sharing, Grey, and communicating. That's part of what love is."

A wicked sparkle entered his gaze. "I'll show you some communication." Boldly he stroked a hand over her bottom and squeezed.

"Grey!" Her admonishment attracted the attention of a few people nearby, reminding her they were in a public place. Heart pounding, she pushed away from him, attempting to skirt his advances. It was just like him to take the edge off their serious conversation with playful overtures, but she truly didn't mind.

"I'm talking about the verbal kind of communication," she chastised in a low voice.

He reached for her again and she tried to elude his grasp. But he was agile and quick and she ended up right back where she'd started. In his arms. He gave her a lascivious look that made her toes tingle. "Yeah, you like it when I get verbal, don't you?"

A thrill of excitement rippled through her. Oh, she did. Shamelessly.

"Ah, Grey." She sighed. Doing what came naturally, she slipped her arms around his neck. She didn't care who glanced their way, because she knew they looked like a couple in love, even if Grey wouldn't admit to such an emotion. "What am I going to do with you?"

"Oh, I'm sure I can think of something," he murmured, wiggling his brows suggestively.

HANDS ON HER HIPS, Mariah scanned the board games stacked on the top shelf in the entryway closet of Mark's mountain house, searching for a way to pass a few hours until bedtime. As busy and enjoyable her afternoon with Grey had been, she wasn't the least bit tired. If anything, after their talk she felt invigorated and hopeful, and nowhere near ready to end an almost-perfect day.

Hearing Grey pad barefoot into the living room from the kitchen, she glanced over her shoulder and watched him set two glasses on the coffee table and pour wine into each. Behind him, a small fire crackled in the hearth, taking the slight mountain chill from the room.

He lifted his head and met her gaze, his mouth quirking in a smile that started a pleasant tickle in the pit of her belly. "What are you doing?"

"I found some games earlier and thought it would be fun for us to play one."

He adjusted the only lamp in the room to low, giving the room an intimate setting. "I vote for strip poker."

She shot him a pointed look. "You know how lousy I am at card games."

"That's what I was counting on," he drawled, a sexy gleam in his eyes.

Shaking her head, but unable to summon any real irritation at his obvious scheme, she glanced back at the flat boxes on the shelf, and spotted one of her favorites. "How about a game of Scrabble?"

He settled himself on the couch. "I've never played before."

"You're kidding?" His serious expression told her he was not. She reached for the game, deciding it was time he learned one of her family's favorite pastimes. "Scrabble is one of those all-American games that never go out of style. It's right up there with Monopoly."

"I've never played Monopoly, either."

She gaped at him, shocked and amazed that someone had survived childhood without the pleasure, fun and frustration of landing on the square that said, "Do Not Pass GO, Go Directly To Jail. Do Not Collect $200." She approached the couch, board game in hand. "How about backgammon?"

"Nope."

"Yahtzee?"

He gave his head a negative shake.

Setting the Scrabble game on the coffee table, she sat on the cushion next to his. "What games *did* you play?"

He handed her a glass of wine and took a long swallow of his own. Finally he said, "I was a whiz at solitaire."

She was certain he was teasing, until she saw a flicker of something truthful and raw in his gaze. *Solitaire.* As in one. As in alone.

She tried to dismiss the swell of compassion filling her

chest, knowing he wouldn't want any part of it. "Your parents never played games with you?"

"My mother was too busy trying to please my father to play games with a child," he said blandly, watching the pale gold liquid swirl in his glass. "And my father wasn't exactly the bonding type."

She took a drink of wine, thinking of her own happy childhood, filled with wonderful memories and an abundance of love and laughter. Her parents had always been there for her and Jade, to support them, guide them and give them the best possible childhood they could. The memories of her youth were fond ones, the kind of memories she hoped to pass on to her own children one day.

"Didn't you do anything as a family?" she asked. "Camping? Barbecues? Going to the beach?"

"Nope. I was lucky if my father showed up for dinner at night and cuffed the back of my head in greeting." His lips slashed into a sardonic smile. "My parents didn't exactly marry under traditional circumstances."

She tucked her legs beneath her, settling closer to him. "What do you mean?"

Grey squeezed his eyes shut and rested his head back on the couch. Damn. She was going to make him exhume old memories. But isn't that what he'd promised her he'd try to do? Give her a piece of his past and share the reasons why marriage and children held little appeal for him?

Blinking his lashes open, he released a tight breath and let the truth spill out. "The reason my parents married is because my mother got pregnant with me. My father owned up to his responsibility, but I learned early on that I was more of an inconvenience to Aaron Nichols than anything else. A reminder of the mistake he'd made and the price he'd had to pay for it."

Mariah looked horrified at the prospect. "Surely your father loved you."

Harsh laughter escaped him. "If he did, I never heard it, nor did he show it." His mother hadn't been one for open displays of affection, either, at least not with him. Oh, he was sure in her own way his mother cared for him, but never had she told him, "I love you," and *he* had never spoken those words. To anyone. How could he when they'd mock everything he'd experienced as a child?

"My father was great at dishing out insults and making me feel worthless," he went on, recounting the events of his childhood. "Like the time I was playing ball with a friend in our front yard and I missed a catch, tripped over my own foot and fell. My father was standing out on the porch watching, waiting for something, anything to give him an excuse to ridicule me. He immediately pounced on my clumsiness and proceeded to bellow out what a clumsy idiot I was for falling on my face and missing such an easy catch. And from there his ranting escalated, as it always did."

Shock transformed Mariah's features and seemed to render her speechless. Well, he wasn't through shocking her yet. Standing, he walked to the fireplace, grabbed the poker and jabbed at the dying embers in the hearth.

"My friend was smart enough to leave, but I had no-where to go. While the neighborhood watched, my father yelled about how I'd never amount to anything and how miserable I made his life. And while my father humiliated me, my *mother* cowered on the front porch and watched the whole thing." His stomach churned at the recollection of his father's verbal abuse, and his mother's weakness and inability to help her child or herself. "Then he grabbed me by the shirt collar and dragged me into the house to dole out more insults."

"Your mother didn't say anything?" she asked incredulously.

He glanced over his shoulder at her, a sardonic grin on his lips. "She never did."

She gasped, her eyes rounding in astonishment. "Why in the world not?"

"My mother was too damned afraid of losing my father, of making him mad. She never said a word, and she never interfered with my father's tirades, even when they were directed at her." And in the end it hadn't matter that she'd been submissive; Vivian Nichols never gained the love she'd craved from her husband, the kind of attention Grey had so desperately wanted from his mother when he'd been a child.

He tossed another log on the fire and watched the sparks filter up the chimney. "When I was a little boy, all I wanted was to please my father, but I learned early on there was no pleasing Aaron Nichols. He was hell-bent on despising me, and taking his anger and hostility out on me and occasionally on my mother."

"You were an innocent child, Grey!"

He gave a shrug stiffer than the casual, who-gives-a-damn gesture he'd been striving for. "Aaron Nichols was a cold, heartless bastard, and to this day I don't understand what my mother saw in him or how she could supposedly love someone so cruel. I swear, it was a blessing in disguise when he died in a car accident."

Except his mother hadn't learned a thing. After a brief grieving period she'd gone on with her quest to find love and acceptance, looking for it in all the wrong places and latching on to any man who seemed the least bit interested in her. Many had used her, a few had married her, but none had loved her the way she was searching for. Unconditionally. Faithfully. Forever.

Grey didn't think there was any such thing.

"Do you still talk to your mother?" Mariah asked quietly.

He went back to poking the logs, just to rid himself of some of his restless energy. "Three times a year," he said emotionlessly, because that's how he felt inside. Empty and hollow. "Her birthday, mine and Christmas. We never seem to have much to say to one another. She's got her life and I have mine."

He heard her sigh regretfully from behind him. "Grey—"

He turned around, his grip tightening on the metal rod in his hand. "My childhood wasn't exactly ideal, was it?" he interrupted, not wanting any of the sympathy she'd been about to offer. He'd come to terms with the reality of his harsh and undesirable childhood long ago. His mother's weaknesses had taught him to be a stronger person, and his father's disregard and vicious insults had made him more determined to be successful in life, even if his achievements hadn't made up for the tiny bit of recognition Grey had sought, and never received as a child.

"No, your childhood was far from ideal," she agreed, an ache in her voice. An ache that matched the one in his chest.

"And it certainly wasn't a great training ground for future fatherhood," he returned. "I have no idea how to act around kids, and I fumble with babies." Returning the poker to its stand, he braced his forearm on the brick mantel. He stared into the crackling fire, gathering the courage to speak his greatest fears aloud. "Do you remember the day in my office when you said that being a parent is a scary proposition?"

"Yes," she said softly, and with tremendous patience.

"Well, you're right about that." He glanced over his

shoulder, meeting her questioning gaze. "Just the thought of raising a child scares the hell out of me." What if he screwed up? What if he was more like his father than he knew?

She gave him a gentle smile, throwing him totally off balance. "I'm sure you'd feel differently with your own."

He jammed his fists into the front pockets of his shorts, his jaw hard. Anger and the need to believe her statement fought a battle within him. "How can you be so certain?"

Uncurling her legs from beneath her, she stood and approached him. Understanding and a deeper emotion shone in her gaze. "Because I know you're kind and caring, and that's what makes a parent a good parent. The rest comes naturally."

He shook his head in denial. "I don't think I want to find out. I don't want kids, Mariah. I never want a child to feel the way I did."

Stepping behind him, she pressed herself against his back and wrapped her arms around his waist. A warmth more comforting than the fire in the grate surrounded him. She rested her cheek on his shoulder and rubbed her palms over his chest and belly. The movement soothed the upheaval tearing him apart inside. "You'd never intentionally hurt a child, Grey."

A lump grew in his throat. Twining his fingers with hers, he lifted her hand, pressed a kiss in her palm, then tugged her around so he held her in his arms. He gazed down at the only woman who'd cared enough about him to search deeper than the surface. He'd given her the hard facts of his childhood and opened up in ways that terrified him. And she'd listened, never once judging him. And even though he still couldn't bring himself to make her any of the promises he knew she wanted to hear, she

was looking at him with an adoration that made his heart swell with an overwhelming emotion.

"Thank you," he whispered, the two words inadequate for the foreign feelings he was experiencing.

A pleased, cat-in-cream smile curled her mouth. "No, thank *you*, for sharing."

He'd fully expected the conversation to put a damper on their evening, but Mariah's eyes had taken on a vivacious sparkle that chased away any gloom that might have lingered.

"Sooo," she purred, a challenging lilt to her voice. She stroked her hands up his chest and around his neck, molding herself intimately to him. "You up for a game of Scrabble? I'm a good teacher and you've always been a quick learner."

He cocked a brow. "I think it's the other way around."

She laughed throatily, the sound thickening his blood and other parts of his anatomy.

He grinned at her playfulness while trying to keep a tight rein on his desire. Damn if she didn't turn him on faster and harder than any carnal fantasy he'd ever had. She *was* his every fantasy come to life, and he wanted her in the worst way. In every way she could imagine. And then some.

He remembered the second promise he'd made her, and groaned in frustration. "Are you sure I can't talk you into strip poker?"

She shook her head, though he swore he saw a flicker of desire in those bright blue eyes of hers. "Nope."

Slipping from his arms, Mariah grabbed his hand and pulled him down to the rug in front of the fireplace, determined to thoroughly enjoy this simple, uncomplicated time with Grey. Within minutes they sat across from one another with the game board between them. They picked

their square tiles, and while she gave him the relatively simple rules to follow he poured them each another glass of wine.

Mariah started the game, displaying the word C-H-I-L-D across the center line of the board. Tallying up her score, she jotted it down on a piece of paper. While she drew five more tile squares he added R-E-N to her word and lengthened it to C-H-I-L-D-R-E-N, giving himself a double-letter score in the process.

"Very clever," she said, scribbling down his higher score. Glancing back at her hand, she chewed on her lower lip, then added I-G-H to the H in CHILDREN to make H-I-G-H.

A slow, sexy grin spread across Grey's face. Without hesitating, he placed a T on top of her HIGH, spelling T-H-I-G-H with a double-letter score.

"You catch on quick," she said wryly, and took a drink of her wine. Studying the board, she added A-S-T below the E in CHILDREN.

"East," Grey murmured thoughtfully as he scanned his letters. Smirking, he laid down his tiles, placing B-R on top of her EAST and an S on the end to give him a double-word score.

"Breasts?" she asked incredulously.

"Hey, it was all I had," he said, holding his hands up in defense. Then his voice lowered, as did his gaze, right to where the buttons on her blouse ended and the dip of her cleavage began. "Besides, I like the word *breasts*."

As if on cue, her breasts swelled and her nipples tingled against lace, ruthlessly reminding her how long it had been since she'd felt the stroke of his hands there, the wet heat of his mouth....

"I'm sure you do, not to mention the eighteen extra points you just tacked on to your score," she groused,

shaking off the need coiling deep in her belly. She shuffled her letters around on her rack, her brow knit in concentration. With a triumphant smile, she added *P-A-R-T-I-N* to the *G* in *THIGH*.

While she fished out new tiles, he played his hand. *O-N-G-U-E* after *PARTING*'s *T*.

Her gaze shot to his, and she automatically dampened her bottom lip with her tongue. He watched her, his eyes growing dark as molten gold. And as hot as the embers in the hearth. *Tongue.* The word brought all kinds of sensual images to mind—the silken glide of his tongue along hers, the lap of his tongue along her neck, then flicking over the peaked tips of her breasts. Thighs, breasts, tongues...

She cleared her throat. "What's with all these body parts?"

The wicked smile tipping his mouth spoiled his attempt at innocence. "Is there a rule against using body parts?"

She busied herself switching tiles around on her rack. "Well, no."

He tipped his head curiously. "So, what's the problem?"

Oh, the rogue knew exactly what the problem was. She should have guessed that he'd put a twist on the game—a game he'd never played, no less!—and succeed in arousing her with a few simple words.

She took a gulp of her wine, hoping the alcohol would take the edge off the growing ache settling in her belly and lower. No such luck, it only increased the heat and need within her. "There's no problem," she said, flashing him a sweet smile.

"Good. Your turn."

Drawing a breath to steady her hand, she arranged her next set of letters, *L-A-Y*, on the board, underneath the *P*

in *PARTING*, spelling the word *P-L-A-Y*. *Let's see him make a body part out of that,* she thought smugly.

He placed *F-O-R-E* on top of her *PLAY*.

She gaped at him in disbelief. The man was good. Too good.

He grinned like the bad boy he was. "Not bad, eh? And I even managed to rack up another twenty-one points." He reached for replacement tiles. "I think I like this game."

Her gaze narrowed. "Are you sure these tiles aren't marked somehow?"

Deep laughter rolled from his chest. "Of course they aren't."

"Are you cheating?"

He shook his head, not at all offended by her accusation. "You set the game up, sweetheart, not me."

Taking a deep swallow of wine, she finished what was left in her glass, finally feeling her body relax. "No one can be so lucky to draw all these sexy words," she complained.

Smothering another grin, he tipped the bottle of wine against her glass and refilled it. "Personally, I think it makes the game more interesting."

She mimicked him beneath her breath. Thinking to throw him off, she jumped to the other side of the board and added *O-C-K* to the *L* in *CHILDREN*.

He smoothly interjected, adding *L-I-P* on top of her *LOCK*.

"Liplock?" A sputter of laughter escaped her. He'd gone too far. "You can't be serious. *Liplock* isn't a word."

He casually picked up new tile squares. "Sure it is."

"Prove it. We need a dictionary. I'm issuing a challenge." She started to her feet, a woman on a mission. No way was she going to let him get away with this one.

He snagged her wrist before she could stand. "I don't need a dictionary, and I'll gladly meet your challenge."

Her pulse raced beneath the thumb stroking the inside of her wrist. "You expect me to go on your say-so?" Her voice was breathless. At the moment she feared she'd believe anything he said.

"Absolutely not." Purpose glittered in his eyes, primitive and wholly sexual. "You want proof that *liplock* is a word, then I'll give it to you." With a gentle tug on her wrist he brought her to her hands and knees, the game still between them. Taking advantage of her surprise, he released her wrist and slid his fingers through her hair, cradling the back of her head in his palm.

Oh, God. She struggled for strength to stop this madness, damning the wine that had slowed her reflexes. She was in trouble. Big trouble.

Leaning forward, he brought their faces inches apart, his expression full of satisfaction. "Take note. In a second our *lips* are gonna *lock*, sweetheart," he murmured huskily. Making good on his promise, he settled his mouth firmly over hers, stealing her breath with exquisite mastery and the slow, erotic glide of his tongue past the seam of her lips.

A shudder rocked through her, and she groaned. Tentatively she let their tongues meet, and they tangled and swirled like long-lost lovers reunited. Then deeper strokes. Bolder forays. She returned the kiss like a woman starved for the taste of her mate, ignoring the warning in her mind to stop, and the melting of her body, priming her for a more intimate act. All that mattered was Grey and the ultimate pleasure of his touch, his kiss.

Closing her eyes, she surrendered to the mindless warmth weakening her limbs. The hand tangled in her hair tightened and the tenor of the kiss changed from

slow seduction to the basic, raw heat of passion. She felt his need, sensed his desire in the sudden, urgent way he slanted his mouth over hers and took complete possession.

Without breaking the hot kiss he moved closer, hitting the playing board with his knee and scattering the letter tiles. Mariah no longer cared about the game. No longer gave a thought to the silly word that had ignited such a wild hunger in the both of them. All that mattered was the hand he'd fitted so snugly over her breast and the emotion she tasted in Grey's kiss, the wanting. *The pure need.*

Mariah's head spun, and she clutched his shirt, holding on as the dizzying sensation threatened to consume her, right along with Grey's delicious kisses. His fingers fumbled with the buttons on her blouse, and she felt a whisper of cool air on her chest as the material parted. He lifted his head, breaking their kiss, and stared at the breasts nestled in satin-and-lace cups, his hands clenching at his sides. The mounds swelled and her nipples tightened beneath his gaze. For weeks she'd resisted him. After what they'd shared today, she wanted to make love with him.

Slowly she reached up and unsnapped the front hook of her bra.

A blunt curse reached her ears. With an impatient sweep of his arm Grey pushed the game board and pieces out of the way then gently eased her down onto the rug in front of the fireplace. He yanked off his shirt, tossed it aside and followed her down, stretching his body over hers.

"God, what you do to me, Mariah," he groaned helplessly, then fitted his mouth to hers once more while his hands tugged her blouse and the straps of her bra over her shoulders. The material bunched around her upper arms, and he left it there, restricting her reach. She

moaned as he rubbed his chest against hers, the friction of hard muscle, a sprinkling of hair, and heat melting the last of her resistance.

He gentled the kiss, giving her slow, drugging strokes of his tongue that tapered into playful bites along her damp lower lip. She tried to touch him, but her hands only reached his sides. A frustrated sound escaped her.

"Shh, baby," he murmured, trailing soft kisses along her jaw and down her neck until, finally, his tongue swept over a taut, aching nipple. Then he drew the pearled tip into his mouth and suckled her deeply.

She cried out, straining against the bonds around her arms until her fingers sank into his thick hair. She held him there while he paid equal attention to each breast. Shifting restlessly, she twined her legs over the back of his thighs and urged him forward. He obliged, burying his face in her neck and rocking his hips against her. She welcomed him, complaining of the clothes separating them. He arched rhythmically and groaned, low and deep. She clamped her legs around his waist, tossed her head back, and gave a great big shudder of need.

Grey clenched his jaw, suppressing the instinctive urge to free the erection straining the fly of his shorts, strip off Mariah's clothes and take her, fast and hard. He'd never meant for things to get so out of control. He'd meant to seduce her, yes, but never had he expected her to be so willing, so eager, not after she'd demanded they not make love this weekend.

But that's exactly what she wanted. He could feel it in the softening of her body, hear it in the panting of her breath. He lifted his head and peered at her flushed face. He could see it in her eyes, smoky with passion.

He swore. This wasn't the romantic reunion he'd envisioned for him and Mariah. True, they'd formed a special

bond today, and as much as he wanted her, he didn't want to take advantage of the situation and jeopardize their fragile truce. Or have her regret making love later, when desire cleared and reality intruded.

"Grey?" she questioned huskily.

Her dreamy and aroused expression threatened his resistance. "We made a deal, remember?" He choked on the words. Damn, she should be reminding *him* of that!

She either didn't remember their pact, or she didn't care. Her fingers found the loops in the waistband of his shorts and tugged impatiently. Thank God she couldn't reach the snap and zipper, or he'd be a goner for sure.

Lifting her head, she nuzzled his throat, sank her teeth gently into his neck, then soothed the love bite with her tongue. He sucked in a quick breath at her brazen display, his heartrate accelerating off the scale. He attempted to move off her, but the fingers caught in his belt loops, the legs tangled around his, held him secure.

A hoarse, helpless laugh erupted from him. "I'm trying real hard to be good here, Mariah, but I need your help."

She whimpered. The softness of want and need in her gaze nearly killed him. He had her right where he'd been trying to get her for over a month. He was a fool to let her go, but he'd be a bigger fool to risk losing her trust. And that meant keeping a promise he'd made. *No making love.*

He brushed her hair away from her face, feeling the quiver of her body beneath his. A quiver from being strung too tight and needing release. He might not be able to slake his own lust, but that didn't mean he couldn't take the edge off hers.

He skimmed a hand over her hip and along the length of silken thigh. "Let me take care of you," he murmured. He knew all it would take was the intimate glide of his fingers between damp folds of flesh, the heat and touch of

his mouth, the soft stroking of his tongue, to give her body the pleasure it sought.

She shook her head and drew a deep breath as if to gather her composure. "No. When we make love, I want you with me all the way."

His pulse stilled. *When*, not *if*. Dare he hope?

She touched his jaw lightly, a tremulous smile lifting her lips. "But for tonight, will you just hold me in your arms?"

Turning his head, he placed a kiss in her palm. "Yeah, I'd like that." He certainly didn't want to spend another night alone.

Moving off her, he gave a grimace as he stood, his aroused body screaming with frustration. He helped her up, adjusted her blouse so he wasn't tempted by her lush curves, and let her have the privacy of the bathroom first.

Ten minutes later, after they'd both changed and their earlier passion had time to cool, Mariah climbed into bed beside Grey and snuggled into his embrace. With a deep sigh that feathered across his chest, her arm draped over his waist, she drifted off to sleep.

Grey remained awake. Stroking Mariah's hair, he reveled in the contentment ribboning through him, a feeling unlike anything he'd ever experienced. One he'd only shared with Mariah.

One thing was for certain. He never wanted the warm, comforting feeling to end.

7

"WHAT TIME ARE WE leaving today?" Mariah asked Grey as he helped her make the bed the following morning. Sunshine streamed through the lace curtains framing the bedroom window, warming her as much as being wrapped in Grey's arms during the night had. She'd missed the intimacy of sleeping with Grey, the way he curled his body around hers from behind, and the possessive way his palm always seemed to find the curve of her breast.

Smoothing her hand over a wrinkle in the quilt, she smiled at the memory of his sweet, nuzzling, good-morning kiss against her neck and his admirable restraint. She'd awoken to the feel of his arousal pressing against her bottom. It would have been so easy for him to shimmy up the nightgown he'd bought her, ease her panties down and slide deep inside where she'd wanted him last night. Where she'd ached for him that morning still.

Sighing, she glanced up at him, wondering if he'd heard her question. He stood at the opposite side of the bed, wearing khaki shorts, a red polo shirt and a determined look. "Grey?"

He picked up one of the throw pillows on the floor beside him and turned it over in his hands. "I was thinking about staying up here a few more days."

"A few more days?" she echoed, frowning. It was Sun-

day, and they both had businesses to run. Starting tomorrow morning.

His shoulders lifted in a casual shrug. "Just until the
end of the week."

"The end of the week!" She came around the bed, unable to believe he'd suggest something so spontaneous
and rash. To her way of thinking, a week constituted more
than just "a few days." They'd shared a wonderful weekend together but they couldn't stay up in Arrowhead forever. "Grey, I don't think that would be such a good
idea."

"I think it's a great idea. My best one yet." He tossed
the pillow against the headboard, and when his gaze met
hers again, the depths were filled with a recklessness that
made her distinctly uneasy. "Mark said I could use the
place as long as I need it, so why not make the most of
things?"

She shook her head. It was unlike Grey to be
so...reckless. "Because I have appointments to keep, clients to see, contracts to go over and sign. *A business to op-
erate!*"

"So do I, but it can all wait a week." He braced his fists
on his hips, his stance firm and unyielding. "I'm willing to
clear my entire schedule for you. For *us.*"

"I can't believe what you're saying!" She paced to the
end of the bed, trying to reason with a man who'd once
been so reasonable. "You can't hold me hostage for a
week—"

"Wanna bet?" A wicked grin curved his mouth as he
slowly moved toward her. "I kinda like the sound of you
being my captive, at my mercy..."

She abruptly stopped, steeling herself against his
words, his advance, that bone-melting, she'd-do-
anything-for-me smile, and held up her hand to ward him

off. "Then you stay and I'll go. Give me the keys to the Jeep," she ordered.

"Search me for them," he dared her, holding his arms wide to give her access to every inch of him. "If you find them, we'll go."

The only thing she would find was a body to die for, and a man who'd enjoyed every minute of the frisking. She sighed in frustration and dragged her hand through her hair. "Why are you doing this?"

Quicker than she could anticipate, he reached out, slid his hand around her neck and brought her mouth to his. He summed up his answer in a deep, emotion-filled kiss that left her breathless, as soft as dew and clinging to him. A kiss so full of need and longing and a thousand other feelings that touched her heart and swept through her soul.

When he finally lifted his head, she stared up at him in a dazed fog, a willing prisoner—if it meant she might gain his love. Oh, Lord, was she wishing for the impossible?

"*That's* why I'm doing this," he said fiercely, his eyes blazing with heat, arousal and something more. He framed her face in his hands, holding her immobile.

As if she planned on going anywhere.

"Maybe sharing *is* all that it's cracked up to be," he said, a lopsided grin canting his mouth. "Something within me shifted this weekend, Mariah. Something that feels wonderful and scares me half to death because I don't understand completely what it is." He pulled in a deep breath, his gaze searching hers. "But whatever it is, I want to explore it with you, without the craziness of work and everyday life interfering. I want more time alone. No interruptions, no outside influences."

She pressed her hands to his chest. "Grey, we can't hide away for another five days, ignore our work, our respon-

sibilities." This time her protest was weak. Anything that had to be done Jade was more than capable of handling. It was a matter of her sister cooperating enough to handle her absence.

"My mind is made up, Mariah." He slid his hands down her back and clasped them at the base of her spine, holding her body, as well as her heart, close. "I'm not giving you a choice."

His caveman routine should have irritated her, but the truth was, she wanted this time alone as much as he did. He was willing to give up so much for her to make their relationship work. How could she refuse?

"We'll go into the village for more food, I'll call Jeanie at home and have her clear my schedule for the week, and you can do the same with Jade."

"Do I have to?" Mariah groaned into his shoulder and squeezed her eyes shut. "Jade is going to disown me."

Grey chuckled, then grew serious. "Jade will survive. What's between us is far more important."

He was right. She, too, had felt something more over the past two days with Grey...hope for the future. Unable to deny him his wish, she slipped from his arms and said, "Let's go make some phone calls."

He swatted her bottom as she passed and grinned when she glared at him from over her shoulder. Then he had the audacity to wink.

"I knew you'd see things my way," he said.

"Like you gave me a choice," she muttered.

"ARE YOU TOTALLY and completely out of your mind?" Jade's disapproving tone drifted through the phone lines to Mariah. "Standing me up on Friday night and skipping town with Grey for the weekend is one thing, but an entire week?"

Mariah was in too good a mood to let her sister's interrogation put a damper on her newfound happiness. "I'm staying, Jade."

"The man has you brainwashed!"

Smiling, Mariah glanced toward the grocery store Grey had slipped into while she made her phone call in a nearby booth. The "man" Jade was referring to had her hopelessly in love. "Stand in for me on whatever appointments you can manage and reschedule the others for the following week," she told Jade. "There's nothing pressing on my desk or in the works, so everything else you can handle or it can wait until I get back."

A long-suffering sigh reached Mariah. "At least give me a number where I can reach you if something comes up."

"*If* the cabin had a phone and I gave you the number, I'm sure I wouldn't get a moment's peace. But there isn't a phone, so I'm in luck."

"How cozy," Jade said, her tone bordering on peevish.

"Actually, it is a nice little romantic retreat," Mariah said, deliberately goading her sister.

Jade made an exasperated sound. "I'm having you committed."

Mariah wound her finger around the phone cord, asking innocently, "Whatever for?"

"Your sanity has *obviously* fled. What else would possess you to run off with Grey for an entire week?"

The answer came easily, Mariah thought. Love had possessed her. And hope. Grey had given her a part of his past he'd never shared with her before. A vulnerable side that touched her and made her optimistic for their future together. He'd shared hopes, broken dreams and fears, and she wanted to reassure and soothe him. In time, and with an abundance of love and patience, she was certain

she could replace those terrors with the knowledge that he'd be a good, loving husband and a better father than his own had been.

Her dad had taught her to fight for what she believed in. She believed in Grey and his ability to let his caring flourish into an emotion far richer and more rewarding. It was all a matter of showing him how wonderful love could be. Making him see that love was a good thing, and nothing at all like the disappointing memories of his childhood.

Another five days alone with him could make all the difference to their future.

"Have all my efforts been for nothing?" Jade asked. "Haven't you learned *anything* I've taught you the past couple of weeks?"

"Like what?"

"Like not to trust a man's motives, for one."

That was Jade's motto, not hers. Besides, Grey had never given her any reason to distrust or doubt him. "I believe Grey's intentions are honorable."

Jade gave a snort of disbelief. "You've slept with him, haven't you?"

"That's none of your business."

"I'll bet he's making you all kinds of promises, isn't he?"

"Not one."

"Well, considering the dreamy quality of your voice, you'd think he offered you a ring and marriage."

Not quite, but close. *If you want the ring, it's yours.* Grey's words echoed through Mariah's mind. Now she just needed a declaration and a proposal to go with it. She was confident she'd have both. Soon.

"I give up, Mariah," Jade said, a sigh of defeat escaping

her. "You're a hopeless cause. The next time Grey breaks your heart, just remember that I told you so."

SITTING ON A LARGE, smooth boulder at the back of Mark's cabin, Grey stared out at the rippling surface of Lake Arrowhead, feeling more content and relaxed than he could ever remember.

It was a beautiful summer afternoon, hot—but a slight breeze and the tall pines surrounding the lake kept the day bearable. Families on vacation played on the lake in their ski boats, and kids floated by Mark's dock on rafts and inner tubes, laughing and frolicking in the cool water.

Casting a quick glance over his shoulder toward the cabin, Grey wondered what was keeping Mariah. She'd promised him she'd be down in a few minutes and he already missed her. He wanted to share every minute with her, make every moment special, and have it last forever. Up in the mountains, away from everyone and everything, anything seemed possible. Even forever.

Picking up a small, flat stone from the ground beside him, he tossed the rock into the lake and watched it skip four times before sinking. He hadn't known what to expect when he'd kidnapped Mariah—it had been a last-ditch desperate effort to persuade her to his way of thinking—but never would he have imagined that her caring and gentleness would change him.

And he was changing. While she'd coaxed him to open up and confide in her about his painful past, a cold, hardened part of him had subsided. Resentments he'd harbored for so long had eased, making room for the more tender emotions Mariah inspired in him. As impossible as it seemed, his feelings for her had altered over the past couple of days, too, growing stronger, richer and infinitely more fulfilling. He felt like the luckiest man on

earth and knew Mariah had everything to do with his newfound elation.

Yet he was hesitant to put a label on the unique emotion settling so warmly in his chest. Love wasn't possible, not for him, yet caring didn't seem like a powerful enough word to describe how he felt, either.

Well, hell.

"Hey, you," Mariah said, sliding onto the rock behind him. She scooted close, bracketing his thighs with her long, bare legs. "What are you doing?"

He turned his head and glanced at her. "Waiting for you."

"Well, I'm here." She smiled and placed an affectionate, kiss on his cheek. "What do you want to do today?"

Looking at those sweet lips so close to his, and feeling her thighs tighten at his hips when she shifted to find a more comfortable position, there was only one answer that sprang to mind. He wanted to spend the entire day making love to her, in bed, on the sofa, out on the deck in nature's glory, in front of a nice, warm fire.... A hundred, erotic scenarios flashed before him, but he'd made her a promise he wasn't about to break, no matter how badly he ached to be physically close to her.

So, instead, he suggested an activity certain to keep his mind off of sex. "I was thinking we could follow one of these trails around Mark's cabin and go hiking."

She shuddered. Wrapping her arms around his waist, she rubbed her palms over his flat belly. "Grey, I'm up here to relax. I refuse to let you torture me that way."

"We'll find an easy trail." Hooking his fingers beneath her knees, he lifted her legs and draped them over his thighs, so her calves were more accessible to his hands. He cupped the firm flesh in his palms and kneaded. "And when we get back we can soak any aches or pains you

might have in the spa. And if that doesn't work, I'd be happy to be your personal masseur."

"Hmm." A tiny sound of pleasure escaped her and she all but melted around him. "Sounds tempting."

Grey nearly groaned at the press of her breasts against his back as she arched, and the way her hands slid to his thighs gave new meaning to the word *temptation*. "Give me a few more minutes, sweetheart, and you'll agree to just about anything I ask."

She laughed into his ear, the sound husky. "I'm just about there."

At that moment, three young, tow-headed boys came barreling down the path from a nearby cabin and onto the dock next to Mark's, forcing Grey to ease up on his seduction, though he didn't stop touching her. The trio hooted and hollered and jumped into the water in a succession of dive-bombs and belly flops, then came back up sputtering to splash one another. Grey chuckled at the rambunctious youths and their antics.

"Umm, that does look like fun, doesn't it?" Mariah asked.

"Feeling a little hot and bothered, are ya?" he drawled lazily. "Like maybe you need to cool off?"

"I'm perfectly fine," she said, giving him a poke in the side to behave himself. "I just meant that those boys look like they're having a good time."

Smiling, Grey watched one boy dunk another. With a war cry, the third kid jumped off the dock and into the water to join in the playful battle. "Yeah, they do."

They watched the boys for a few quiet minutes, then Mariah asked, "Did you ever miss not having a brother or sister to play with while you were growing up?"

"How can you miss something you've never had?" There was enough cynicism in his voice to contradict the

casual shrug of his shoulders. Thankfully, Mariah didn't call him on it. More times than he cared to recall as a child he'd wished for a brother or sister, someone to play with and share secrets. Someone who would have been there for him, just as he would have been around for them, to make them feel wanted, cared for and maybe even loved.

Which had been a foolish whimsy…the selfish longings of a youth searching for acceptance and attention. He hadn't had much experience in feeling wanted, cared for and loved. What made him think he could offer a sibling a part of himself he didn't have to give?

Mariah laughed as one of the boys pushed another into the water, then the third snuck up from behind to shove him in. "I can't imagine what my childhood would have been like without Jade."

"Probably very peaceful and quiet," Grey said wryly.

"And lonely," she added softly.

"Yeah," he agreed, the word *lonely* summing up his entire childhood. "Did you two get along?"

"Not always," she admitted, amusement and sisterly affection in her voice.

He trailed a finger up her leg and beneath her knee, tickling the sensitive flesh there. She shivered and sighed. "Sibling rivalry?" he guessed.

"No, we never really competed. We fought and argued over stupid stuff, like who got the bathroom first and whose turn it was to do the dishes. And Jade was forever borrowing my clothes and not returning them." She gave a growl of frustration that lacked any real annoyance. "She'd swear she never took them, and I'd find whatever it was that was missing in her closet months later. She's one of the most disorganized persons I know."

"And I'm sure *you* never did anything wrong."

"I was a complete angel," she replied primly.

"Till I got hold of you." His voice dropped to a low, sexy rumble.

"Hmm." Her mild response told him that she'd willingly let him corrupt her. "No matter what, though, Jade was always there for me when I needed her. She still is. I wouldn't trade her friendship for anything, even though she does tend to get on my nerves from time to time." She propped her chin on his shoulder. "There's nothing like a sibling's love and friendship. You missed out on something special, Grey."

"And a brother or sister missed out on a lot of hurt and dejection." His voice was harsher than he'd intended.

His edge of anger didn't stop her from pursuing the sensitive subject of his childhood. "You didn't have much fun as a kid, did you?"

"Like I told you the other night, my parents weren't exactly the type to interact with children, or to have 'fun.' We never went anywhere as a family, and I didn't have many friends because my father always scared them off."

"It doesn't have to be that way. Not with your own children. Look at how much fun siblings can have together." She waved a hand toward the dock and the boys playing there. "Wouldn't you just love to watch children of your own grow up, have fun—be a part of their lives? And give them wonderful memories to share with their own children one day?"

He didn't answer, just kept watching the boys. How could he give children memories when he didn't have the first clue how to *make* them?

"I want that, Grey," she went on, her arms tightening around his waist. "I want kids, and I want to give them fun, laughter and even the lessons that come with the right kind of discipline. I'm sorry you never had the playful times, the laughter, the closeness."

Grey squeezed his eyes shut, trying just as hard to shut out the emotions swirling within him. He wanted to tell her not to pity him. And that he'd never chance subjecting a child to the kind of verbal and mental abuse he'd suffered.

A tall blond man strolled down the path the boys had taken earlier. He glanced toward the rock where he and Mariah sat, gave them a neighborly grin and waved, then headed toward the dock, yelling, "Come on, boys, your mother has lunch ready."

"Aw, Dad," one complained, "we haven't been in the water that long!"

"Do we have to?" another said.

"We're not done playing yet!" said the third, then pushed his brothers into the lake and dive-bombed after them. Grey clearly expected their father to get upset, but instead he laughed and let them play a few minutes longer. One of the boys climbed up the ladder onto the dock while his father was talking to one of his brothers. The youngster whooped, ran full force into the bigger man, and they both went tumbling into the water. From there, an all-out water war ensued.

The fun they were having was infectious, and Grey found himself chuckling, too, which eased the lingering tension from his conversation with Mariah. Finally their father insisted they get out and head back to the cabin, before their mother strung every one of them up.

After more grousing and a promise from their dad to return to the lake once they ate lunch and rested, the foursome disappeared up the path.

Wanting to experience some of that spontaneous fun, Grey pulled off Mariah's leather sandals and let them fall to the ground. Then he wrapped his forearms around and beneath her thighs and stood. The abrupt move made her

squeal in alarm. She looped her arms around his neck to keep from falling, and hooked her legs tight around his waist. He toed off his own shoes, and proceeded to carry Mariah toward the dock, piggyback-style.

"Grey?" she asked uneasily. "What are you doing?"

Anticipation filled him with every step he took closer to the water. "I thought we might play a little."

She laughed happily, the sound warming Grey's heart. "I have to warn you," she said, her tone light and mischievous. "I've had more experience at this than you, and you might come out the loser."

Grey didn't know how he could possibly lose, not when he was already having a great time. "I'll take my chances," he said, and jumped off the dock and into the summer-warmed lake. The last thing he heard before they went under was Mariah's name on his lips, and his own wicked chuckles.

They came up laughing and absolutely drenched. As Grey took a great gulp of air, he got shot in the face with a spray of water from Mariah. He coughed, and she giggled, saying, "I told you so."

He dove after her, dunking them both beneath the water. From there, time lost meaning as Mariah showed him how to have fun, how to laugh and how to make memories.

8

MARIAH TOOK A BITE of the raspberry crème brûlée Grey fed to her and moaned in appreciation as the sinfully rich dessert filled her mouth. She sat next to Grey in a cozy, intimate booth at the back of an elegant, expensive restaurant overlooking Lake Arrowhead. A taper candle burned in the center of their table, casting a warm, golden hue around them. They were surrounded by dining couples, but catching the wicked, I-want-to-eat-*you*-up-for-dessert look in Grey's eyes, she wished they were back at the cabin alone.

"This wasn't necessary, you know. Dinner at an exclusive restaurant, a new dress, the roses," she said, still reeling from his very spontaneous suggestion to eat out, and the mini shopping spree he'd taken her on to dress for the occasion. But then again, since their escapade down at the dock two days ago, he'd been full of wonderful surprises.

"Trust me," he said, a lopsided grin canting his mouth as he watched her take another spoonful of brûlée. "It was *very* necessary. I'm tired of frozen meals and deli food. Roses make you smile. And you look better than a dream in that dress." His gaze roved over the garment in question, a form-fitting, pink cashmere sheath that dipped low in the back and ended midthigh. "What I'd like to know is, what are you wearing underneath that dress? Or rather, what aren't you wearing?" Boldly, he skimmed a

hand over her hip, up the side of her ribs until his fingers brushed the curve of her breast.

She sucked in a breath, shocked that he'd be so brazen, though they sat at such an angle the other nearby patrons couldn't see what he'd just done. Her breasts instantly swelled, and her nipples peaked and pushed against the soft material.

"You're not wearing a bra, are you?" His voice was a soft, accusing murmur that slid down her spine like a languid caress.

Feeling reckless enough to join in the game of seduction he'd been playing all week, she dipped her finger in the dessert and brought it to his mouth. "The dress is made to be worn without one," she said, painting his bottom lip with the decadent dessert. "Are you curious about what else I might not be wearing underneath the dress?"

His gaze darkened, and he grasped her wrist before she could pull her hand away. Slowly sucking her finger into his mouth, he swirled his tongue over the tip. She nearly jumped out of her skin when his free hand flattened on her knee and began a leisurely journey upward, disappearing beneath the hem of her dress.

His fingers grazed the lace band of the stockings she'd bought for herself at the boutique in town, then brushed the inside of her thigh, gently coaxing them apart. And damned if her body didn't respond. "Grey..." She wasn't sure if his name was a warning or a whispered plea.

A wicked smile curved his mouth, and he leaned closer, blocking everyone and everything from her view but the heat and desire in his eyes. "I could find out right here, right now, exactly what you are or aren't wearing beneath this dress." His voice had changed, grown husky and enticing. There was a tension in his body, a restless sexual

energy that brought her to full awareness of him and only him.

Remembering the way he'd so easily seduced her out on the terrace at her father's party, she didn't doubt that Grey would make good on his promise now, despite where they were. A week of being around him and sharing an emotional closeness they'd never had before, sleeping with him but not making love, was taking its toll on both of them.

His finger traced the elastic band of her panties along her hip, then dipped lower, following the barrier to the crease between her thighs. "Umm, you *are* wearing panties, but that's hardly a deterrent." To prove his point, he stroked along the silky material covering her mound, rubbing her intimately, making her quiver and ache for the exquisite, erotic sensations she knew he could evoke.

She bit her bottom lip to keep back a groan, and he smiled, a slow, cocky, satisfied grin. Horrified that she was on the brink of succumbing to him once again, she clamped her legs together, trapping his hand between her thighs.

"Can I get you two anything else?"

Mariah's started at the sound of their waiter's voice from behind Grey's shoulder. Her heart thundered in her chest and her face burned in pure mortification, though Grey was positioned in front of her in such a way that it appeared as if they were having an intimate, private conversation and nothing more. But she knew better, because Grey was enough of a scoundrel to remind her by lightly skimming his thumb along the bare skin between the band of her stocking and her panties.

He glanced over his shoulder at the young man. "Just the check, but feel free to take your time about it," he said

pleasantly. "My girlfriend and I are in the middle of a very intriguing conversation."

With a promise to be back shortly, the waiter left their table to tend to nearby patrons. Grey glanced back at her.

She stared into his golden eyes, shivering at the dare still flickering in their depths. "Remove your hand," she said in a hushed voice.

He blinked lazily and made no move to obey her order. "You started this," he murmured.

"And now I'm *ending* it."

"*My* ending would be much more satisfying."

She didn't doubt that. Not for a minute, and not when her body throbbed with a need so fierce she was tempted to let him do whatever he wished.

"Open your legs, sweetheart," he said in a husky, coaxing tone.

"Grey!" she hissed in admonishment.

He chuckled, which infuriated her more. "I can't remove my hand when my fingers are trapped between your thighs."

"Oh." Face warming once again, she relaxed her legs and he pulled his hand from beneath her dress. He smoothed the hem down and leaned back to his own side of the booth just as a small band of waiters sauntered up to a nearby table, delivered a small cake and broke out into the "Happy Anniversary" song for the elderly couple sitting there. Once the applause subsided and the waiters dispersed, Mariah took advantage of the distraction and addressed the couple.

"How long have the two of you been married?" she asked.

The older, distinguished-looking man gazed adoringly at his petite and still beautiful wife. "Forty-eight wonderful years."

The woman sitting by his side blushed becomingly. "And I'd do it all over again in a heartbeat."

The man smiled and gave his wife a sweet kiss. "You know I'm going to remind you of that whenever you're mad at me for something."

The woman laughed, a sound of happiness and delight. "You usually do, honey."

"Well, congratulations," Mariah said before returning her attention to Grey, who was watching the exchange with a small frown marring his brow.

Mariah braced her elbows on the table, propped her chin on her laced fingers and sighed. "Isn't that romantic, being in love after all those years?"

Skepticism shone in his eyes. "It's amazing to think that two people can *stay* together for forty-eight years. But I can hardly believe they're still in love."

"Of course they are," she refuted. She could sense the tension rising in Grey, but she wasn't about to let it dissuade her from pursuing a very important issue. A deep, scarring, emotional issue that could make or break their future. "Why else would they stay married?"

He toyed with the stem of his empty wineglass. "People stay married even though they aren't in love for numerous reasons."

"Such as?" she persisted mildly.

"Obligation. Companionship. I suppose people grow comfortable with one another and know what to expect from the relationship." He glanced at his watch impatiently and muttered, "Where's the damn check?"

Mariah wasn't about to let Grey get out of this one. "You only need to look at that couple to know they're still in love." *It showed in every cherished glance, every tender touch. It was what her grandparents and parents shared. It was what she wanted from her own husband. It was what she so des-*

perately wished she could share with the mule-headed man sitting beside her.

Grey narrowed his gaze at the two people across the way. "I have to say I've seen that look on my mother's face with her numerous boyfriends and husbands," he said cynically. He glanced back at her, his expression shrewd. "So tell me, what's the difference between true love and wanting to be loved so badly you see it even when it's not there?"

Mariah heard the hurt and anger in Grey's voice, even though he'd outright deny any of the bitter emotions. "Sometimes people marry for the wrong reasons," she admitted. "Divorce is always possible, but it all depends on the foundation upon which couples marry. There has to be a strong commitment, and the willingness of the couple to make it work."

The check arrived at that moment, and Grey used the interruption to his benefit. He withdrew enough cash from his wallet to pay the bill and leave a substantial tip. Without a word, he slid from the booth, waited for Mariah to proceed him, then ushered her to the entrance of the restaurant with his hand resting lightly on the small of her back.

Mariah's heart grew heavy on the quiet drive back to the cabin. Grey didn't believe in love because he'd never experienced the emotion. And she was beginning to despair that he'd never open himself to an emotion that would leave him exposed and vulnerable, as he had so many times as a child. He was afraid of being hurt, of being rejected, of giving of himself so completely and then losing in the end.

It was the only way he knew, and it was up to her to show him differently.

By the time they entered the cabin, Mariah had made a

very important decision, and could only hope her plan didn't backfire.

Dropping her purse on the couch, she snapped on the lamp, then turned to Grey. "Would you mind making a small fire?" she asked. Although the day had been warm, the evenings in the mountain were cool.

He headed toward the fireplace without comment and began tossing logs onto the grate. He stoked the fire, giving the task more attention than it deserved. She hated the tension between them after how well their retreat had gone, but knew it was going to get a lot more stressful before the evening was over.

Taking a deep breath to calm her nerves, she stepped up behind Grey. "You told me your mother has been married numerous times, but isn't it entirely possible that she *did*, in some way, love every man she married?"

He set the brass poker back in its stand and straightened, facing her. "Yeah, to the exclusion of everything and everyone else. Including *me*, a stupid little kid who wanted a little affection from his mother so badly that he all but begged for it. My mother lived in a fairy-tale world, Mariah, and she was looking for a prince to take her away from the drudgery of everyday life. Any man who paid her the least bit of attention after my father died became her newest knight in shining armor, whether he wanted to be or not. My mother wouldn't know *love* if it bit her in the ass!"

Mariah calmly stepped out of her sling-back pumps. "Then what is *your* perception of love?"

He moved to the cabin's small wet bar, grabbed a half-empty bottle of scotch and poured himself a healthy portion. "You know how I feel about love." He lifted the drink to his lips.

She intercepted the glass before he could taste a drop

and set the liquor out of reach. He scowled darkly, but she merely smiled. They'd come too far for her to let him shut her out now, or for him to find comfort in a bottle when she was more than willing to comfort him. Physically and emotionally.

"Humor me," she said, tugging on the knot of the tie he'd bought for dinner until the strip of silk loosened. "*If* you believed in love, which we both know you don't, what do you imagine that emotion would encompass?"

He jammed his hands on his hips and glowered at her. "I don't want to get all philosophical about this, Mariah."

"Okay," she said easily, and tossed his new tie somewhere over her right shoulder. She undid the first three buttons on his shirt, deciding to broach things in a less threatening way. "Then tell me, what is your opinion of our relationship?"

His gaze narrowed sharply, and he stiffened. "How do you mean?"

"After nine months, why are we still together?" she asked softly. "What is it that attracts you to me and has made our relationship last this long?"

"Mariah—"

Curling an arm around his neck, she rubbed seductively against him, like a cat looking for some attention. "It must be a purely physical thing between us then," she all but purred.

His gaze darkened and he visibly clenched his teeth. Oh, he was attracted on a physical level all right, and getting more aroused with every slow caress of her body along his. "You know that's not the *only* thing that attracts me to you."

She feigned a pout. "How do I know *anything* if you won't tell me?"

Grey blew out a stream of breath, unable to think when

Mariah was plastered against him so provocatively. Planting his hands firmly on her waist, he stopped the gyrating of her hips. As he stared into soft blue eyes hazy with desire, he realized that he'd never told her just how much she meant to him. Maybe it was something he needed to say, and something she needed to hear.

"I'll make it real simple for you," she said with a slow slide of her tongue across her bottom lip. "What words would you use to describe our relationship?"

He closed his eyes, the words she was asking for jumbling in his mind. He sorted them out, then let his lashes drift open, a peaceful feeling curling through him. Brushing his knuckles along her soft cheek, he gave her the words she sought. "Understanding, caring, respect, trust—" he let a wolfish grin lift his lips "—and a whole lot of lust."

She laughed joyfully. "You love me."

"I didn't say that," he said, his tone cautious.

She smiled knowingly. Triumphantly. "Oh, Grey, you didn't have to. You just described the exact way I feel about you. Those emotions *are* love."

He wanted to deny her claim, but found he couldn't. Or maybe he didn't want to. Damn. He didn't know anymore.

She grasped his hand and led him back to the rug in front of the fireplace, where a small fire crackled and sent out waves of toasty heat. She left him standing there to turn off the lamp. The soft, warm glow of firelight illuminated the curves of her body wrapped in cashmere and shone off the sassy length of her hair.

Their eyes locked, and he eased out a strangled breath. His hands curled into fists at his side. The smile on her lips was sultry and teasing; the look in her eyes seared his soul. He was bewitched, transfixed and so full of strange

emotions he didn't understand. All he understood was the fierce ache to touch her, to ease her to the floor and let his hands and lips worship every inch of her.

Oh, so leisurely, she lifted her hands and pulled down the shoulders of her dress, revealing pale, firm breasts, their centers dark, and her nipples tight. The silky soft material slid down her arms and caught on the swell of her hips. With a slow, provocative shimmy the garment slithered down her long legs and pooled around her feet, leaving her scantily clad in pink lace panties sheerer than a sigh, and those thigh-high opaque stockings he'd discovered earlier, a delicate lace band holding them securely in place.

His heart pounded in his chest and his blood rushed through his veins like liquid fire. Breathing became impossible. He was about to have a heart attack, he was sure.

"Mariah?" Her name escaped on a tight croak. "What about your deal?"

"I'm reneging." She started toward him, her smile as seductive as the sway of her hips. "I'm going to *show* you what love is, just in case you have any lingering doubts in that mind of yours."

All doubts fled the minute her hands landed on his chest and smoothed aside the open vee of his shirt until it tightened around his biceps. He attempted to reach for her, heard the rip of material as he stretched his arms, and realized that she'd effectively turned the tables on him. He couldn't reach her.

He caught the gleam of satisfaction in her eyes seconds before she leaned into him, nuzzling her mouth against his neck. He groaned, his body shuddering as her tongue tasted and her teeth scraped along his throat. Her palms were cool against his heated flesh, seeking, searching and finding his nipples, then lower, skimming along the taut

flesh of his belly. The buttons on his shirt hindered her exploration, and she let out a frustrated sound. Then, to his dazed amazement, she grabbed the sides of his shirt and yanked, sending the buttons flying across the room.

He stared, momentarily speechless. *Damn.* Mariah knew how to please him well and good in bed, turning him on with her sensual responses and her eagerness to discover different variations of making love. She'd initiated sex plenty of times, but he couldn't recall her ever being so assertive, so sexually persuasive in her pursuit of what she wanted.

And what she wanted was his love.

He shook his head, confusion swirling with the drugging lure of desire. "Mariah, baby..."

She gently pushed him backward, until his shoulders pressed against the wall beside the hearth. Before he could issue another word her mouth covered his and she gave him the silkiest, sexiest French kiss he'd ever tasted. Denying his need for her became a distant thought.

Shrugging out of his shirt, he pulled her body tight against his and ran his hands over whatever bare, warm flesh he could. He came up against the barrier of her panties and growled impatiently, though his fingers managed to find their way under the elastic band and skim over a soft thatch of damp curls.

She broke their kiss and pushed away his hands, her breathing ragged. "Not yet, Grey. I'm not through with you."

"Not through?" The question wheezed out of him. What else did she intend to do to him?

She shook her head and smiled softly. "I don't think you quite understand just how much I love you. I want to give you all the love I feel for you in my heart. I want to give you all the love you've never had."

And in that moment, he wanted it, too.

"Let me love you." She placed lingering kisses along his shoulder and lower, where her tongue swirled around his nipple. She whispered in the shadowed room, "You taste so good," before sinking to her knees in front of him.

His breath left him in a tight whoosh of air, deflating his lungs. She pressed her mouth to the taut muscles rippling in his belly, then tossed her head back and held his gaze while she worked his belt loose and lowered his zipper. She pulled his slacks and briefs down, and he sprang free, fully, painfully erect. She swept the garments off, along with his shoes and socks, and tossed them aside, leaving him completely naked and more restlessly inflamed than he'd ever been before.

Her hands skimmed up his tense thighs and over his hips, her thumbs grazing that jutting, masculine part of him that wanted her touch more than he wanted his next breath.

His wish became reality. Her fingers circled his swollen shaft and stroked him. Closing his eyes, he tangled his fingers in her silky hair, groaning at the pleasure consuming him.

She wasn't done driving him insane. The wet heat of her mouth enveloped him, velvet soft and wicked as sin. He gritted his teeth, his body jerking and shuddering in warning.

He swore bluntly. "Stop," he rasped, pulling her back up the length of him. Framing her face in his hands, he kissed her while backing her toward the rug before the fire. Finally he released her, watching as she lowered herself to the floor and lay back, then lifted her hips to remove her panties. She dropped the flimsy piece of material onto the floor, then parted her legs, still clad in those sexy stockings, to make room for him in between. The

firelight made her skin golden, made her eyes fever bright with emotion. He'd never seen such an enticing, erotic vision, and his body responded with a demanding, powerful surge of need.

She touched the swell of her breast, ran her fingers lightly over her belly. "Love me, Grey," she whispered huskily.

Oh, man, how could he not? The thought came up out of nowhere, startling him. But it felt good and right, and he didn't fight it. For the moment, for the night, he'd give her anything she asked.

Settling himself over her, he locked their hands at the side of her head. "Tell me you're still on the Pill," he said desperately, his body quaking with a need he'd be hard-pressed to deny. "Because I didn't bring any condoms with me."

She curled her legs around the back of his thighs and urged him forward, where she was hot and wet and ready for him. "It's safe," she whispered.

His body shuddered in relief. Staring into her dark blue eyes, he slowly pushed into her tight, welcoming sheath. They shared a mutual groan of pleasure, and she arched with a sharp gasp and raised her knees around his waist, taking him deeper and deeper still with every measured stroke.

Despite how many times he'd made love with her, he suddenly couldn't get enough of her, couldn't get deep enough inside her. He wanted to be a part of her, in every elemental way that mattered. Heart, body and soul.

Love. Oh, God, no.

The awesome emotions within him unraveled, breaking on a wave so powerful his body shuddered. He thrust hard and fast, triggering a breathless cry from Mariah as

they both reached the peak and soared over the crest together.

When he regained a normal breathing pattern he moved off Mariah and pulled her close to his side, cradling her in his arms. She buried her face in his neck and let out a long, content sigh.

"I love you," she murmured.

He closed his eyes and swallowed hard, afraid to speak the words she longed to hear.

9

HE LOVED HER.

Mariah made good on her promise to eliminate any lingering doubts from his mind. For the next two days Grey had denied the inevitable. Then he'd come to terms with the fact that the emotions he felt for Mariah were exactly what she'd labeled them. Love. What else could explain the heart-pounding thrill when he was with her, the frenzy of emotions when she looked at him in that soft way of hers or the huge ache of missing her when they were apart for the shortest amount of time?

No other woman had ever evoked such a myriad of emotions from him, but then he'd never remained with one woman long enough to allow anything stronger than a physical attraction to develop. But Mariah... Well, from the very first he'd seen something different in her, a special, caring quality that had drawn and captivated him. Since her, he'd found no other woman could compare in strength, intelligence, beauty and stubbornness.

Smiling, Grey turned his Jeep Cherokee onto the narrow street that wound its way up to the cabin. He'd slipped out almost two hours earlier to get dinner while Mariah had been napping—a well-earned rest after an afternoon of the most emotionally and physically satisfying lovemaking he'd ever experienced. He'd intended to pick up a quick bite at a deli in the village and return before she woke, but as he'd passed that jewelry store they'd

seen last weekend, he'd stopped and made an impulsive purchase certain to convey the feelings in his heart.

Love. As he reflected on the course of his relationship with Mariah, he realized that he'd loved her almost from the beginning. His heart had known, but his mind had refused to acknowledge all the obvious signs. As a direct result of Mariah's determination to make him face past resentments and see his emotions for what they were, his heart and mind were finally in harmony.

And the knowledge scared the hell out of him.

Braking to a stop in front of the cabin, he killed the engine and stared at the darkened structure. Despite the fact that he admitted to loving Mariah, he couldn't help but wonder how long this wonderful feeling would last. Another week? Another month? A year or two? How long would it be before Mariah realized he truly wasn't the marriageable type? That he wasn't the kind of man to love and nurture children? His edges were too rough, his soul too jaded to think he was equipped to handle a child's needs.

He had no ready answers for any of the questions he'd asked himself. All he knew was that for now, he wanted to savor and enjoy the precious commodity he'd found in Mariah. He wanted to share time with her, love her, and when it ended, part as friends and have no regrets. It was as much as he was willing to give, for her sake as much as his own. Certainly after their week together and everything they'd shared, she understood the reasons why he couldn't give her marriage and a family.

But he was willing to offer her the strongest commitment he knew, one that came straight from his heart and soul. After the closeness they'd established, and the love he was willing to declare, he was confident she would say yes this time to his proposal.

Grabbing their dinner, he slid from the vehicle and headed up the walkway. It was dark inside the cabin, but he smiled when he heard the shower running. He debated on joining Mariah, but decided they'd never eat if he offered to scrub her back. Considering they hadn't had a meal since breakfast, they needed nourishment.

In the kitchen, he unpacked their dinner, a small feast of large peeled shrimp, cocktail sauce, fresh croissants and pasta salad. He set one place setting, then lit the votive candle he'd found in the cupboard and placed it in the center of the table. Slipping his surprise beneath a paper napkin just to the side of the one plate, he turned off the light, settled in the high-back wooden chair and waited....

Less than ten minutes later, he heard Mariah come out of the bathroom and call out tentatively. "Grey?"

"In the kitchen," he said, and drew a deep breath that caught in his throat when she glided through the door.

Dressed in scarlet red silk and lace that revealed more than it covered, and bathed in candlelight, Mariah was a vision of temptation. Floral, see-through lace shaped her breasts and swept in a diagonal slash to her left hip. Silky material draped to her ankles in soft cascading folds, but it was the thigh-high slit that captured his attention and made him wonder if she was wearing any panties.

She wasn't supposed to have found the negligee he'd purchased on a whim, but he was glad as hell she had. Swallowing hard, he managed a strangled, "Hi."

"Hi, yourself," she said, her voice husky. She moved toward him, hips swaying, the creamy expanse of thigh peeking and retreating enticingly through that wicked slit.

Blood pooled low in his lap and his body tightened in a subtle, but unmistakable way. She looked sexy, feminine and more provocative than a dream. The hair piled on top

of her head in a loose knot made his fingers itch to pull out the pins and run his fingers through the silky strands.

"I was putting away our clothes and came across this gown," she said, stopping just beyond his reach. She dampened her bottom lip with her tongue and ran a finger lightly down the sheer, scalloped lace outlining her full breasts that nearly spilled from the bodice. "Unless you have a fetish I don't know about, I'm assuming you bought it for me?"

"Yes." He watched her breasts swell from her touch, and her nipples thrust against the lace. His mouth watered. "You fill it out much better than I ever could."

She smiled, tracing that same wicked finger along the strip of lace slashing to her hip. "Did you buy it when you bought me that peach chemise?"

A loaded question. He remembered that she'd expected a nightgown like this one from him that first night, and although he'd given her the conservative chemise, his thoughts had been on the red, racy number. "Guilty as charged."

She tsk-tsked him, and touching the thigh exposed by the slit, she trailed her fingers upward. His anxious gaze followed. "You're a bad boy, Grey Nichols."

"Very bad," he agreed. And feeling more naughty with each passing second. The things he wanted to do to her went beyond illicit and carnal...and she seemed more than willing.

She attempted to look thoughtful, but came across as a sultry vixen instead. "I'll have to think of a fitting punishment."

His heart leapt in anticipation, that wild, tempestuous feeling called love swirling within him. "Trust me, sweetheart, just looking at you in that scrap of nothing is pure torment."

"Good," she purred. "Then all you get to do is look."

His brows rose. She had to be kidding.

She wasn't. Closing the distance between them, she draped herself across his lap. He groaned as her soft fanny nestled against his straining erection, and he automatically caressed his fingers up that tempting, silken thigh.

"No touching," she said, promptly removing his wandering hand, "until I tell you you can."

He gave her a pained look, certain he would never survive her hands-off policy.

She looked over the feast displayed on the table. Dipping a shrimp in cocktail sauce, she lifted it to his lips. "How repentant are you?"

"Very." He took the shrimp into his mouth, then caught her wrist when she would have gone back for another, intent on showing her just how contrite he was. His tongue curled around each finger and lapped the sensitive skin in between, licking away any traces of the sauce. And he took his time doing so, until her eyes grew dark and smoky with arousal, and her breathing became ragged.

He smiled, and nibbled the tip of her finger. "I'm suffering like I've never suffered before."

"Umm." She wiggled on his lap, her lashes falling to a drowsy, sensual half-mast at the proof of his suffering. "I believe you, and because you're so obviously in anguish over your naughty behavior, I'll grant you one touch."

Taking his hand, she settled it on her knee, then guided his flattened palm along the opening in the slit. Her legs parted and her body strained toward the fingers inching along, luxuriating in the pleasure of her soft, bare skin and...no panties. His fingers slid intimately, deeply.

They groaned and shuddered at the same moment— she in pleasure, he in excitement.

"You're *very* good, Grey," she said huskily.

The double entendre wasn't lost on him. "Let me show you how good," he murmured.

Lifting his hand, he gently cupped her cheek in his palm then slowly stroked down her throat and over her shoulder. He held her sexy-soft gaze as he slipped his fingers beneath the wispy strap holding up the bodice of her gown and pushed it down her arm. One lacy cup fell away from the full weight of her breast, and he covered the mound with his palm, plumping the firm flesh, manipulating the nipple into a tight bead he ached to flick with his tongue, draw deeply into his mouth...

"So good." She sighed. Her head rolled back and she arched into his hand, groaning when he rolled her nipple between his fingers. "So bad..."

He chuckled, the sound as strained as the fly on his shorts. "Am I forgiven?"

Her mouth curled into a shameless grin. "I haven't decided yet."

Oh, man, he loved this woman and knew in his heart he'd never tire of her sass, her fire. Knowing there would never be a more perfect opportunity than this moment to express his feelings, he removed his hand from her breast and lifted the strap back to her shoulder, covering her. She gave him a look full of confusion and unquenched desire, while he withdrew the small, square velvet box he'd hidden beneath the napkin.

Grasping her hand, he pressed it into her palm. "Maybe this will help you decide."

She glanced expectantly from the gift, to him. "What's this for?"

"You."

"Why?" Her tone was as skeptical as her expression. "It's not my birthday."

He settled his arms around her, trying to calm the sudden racing of his heart. Damn, but he was nervous. "Does it need to be your birthday for me to give you something to show you how much..." He cleared his tight throat and tried again. "How much I love you?" The words, spoken for the first time, sounded rusty to his own ears.

She stared in disbelief. "What did you say?"

She was going to make him say it again. He supposed he ought to get used to it. "I said...I love you."

Once her obvious shock wore off, tears of happiness filled her eyes. "Oh, Grey, I knew you did."

He gave her a lopsided grin. "You mean I'm going through all this fanfare for nothing?"

"Oh, no," she assured him with a watery smile. She sniffled and brushed at a tear that escaped the corner of her eye. "This is one of the happiest days of my life."

His chest swelled with those strange, tender emotions. She was so easy to please, he thought. And making her happy brought him great satisfaction, like none he'd ever experienced. "Then stop crying and open the box."

Tentatively, she did, and gasped when she saw the ring—a flat band encrusted with rubies and an elegant, one-carat marquis diamond set in the center.

He gently touched her chin, closing the mouth that had dropped open. "I guess the ring speaks for itself, huh?"

"It's absolutely beautiful," she whispered.

Yeah, he thought so, too. The ring was simple in design and far less extravagant than the one they'd seen displayed in the jewelry store window, but the bright rubies had reminded him of Mariah's fire and spirit.

After their argument last weekend, he'd purposely steered clear of the bridal sets at the jewelry store. He'd wanted something personal and intimate, not necessarily a ring, but the clerk had assured him that a ring such as

this one would undoubtedly express his feelings for his girlfriend in a way no bracelet or necklace could. Against his better judgment, he'd given in and purchased the ruby-and-diamond band.

Considering the elation etched on Mariah's face, he gave the clerk credit for knowing her business and the secret desires of women, too.

Taking the band from its nest of crushed black velvet, he took Mariah's left hand and slipped it on her ring finger, marking her as his. The spark of possessiveness he felt at that moment surprised him, but he wasn't about to analyze it. "You make me happy, Mariah. Happier than I've ever been."

She laughed joyfully and hugged him tight, a gesture he returned and savored. Finally she loosened her hold, letting her fingers sift through his hair.

Their gazes locked. "You truly love me?" she asked in awe.

"Didn't you tell me I did that night you seduced me?" he teased.

She gave the hair at the back of his head an affectionate tug. "Yes, you big oaf, but do you *really* believe it?"

Sensing her need for confirmation, he grew serious. "Yeah, I believe it. Being in love scares the hell out of me, but I'm hoping I'll get used to the feeling."

Her mouth curled into a sultry smile laced with triumph. "You will," she murmured. Sliding a hand around to cup his jaw, she urged his mouth up to hers. "I'll make sure of it."

Her lips were warm and soft upon first contact, her mouth sweet and generous when it opened to meet the glide of his tongue. The kiss was slow and lazy, but before long the tenor changed, growing more hungry and urgent

as hands began to wander and the fragile emotions surrounding them mingled with desire.

The kiss went on and on, priming them both for a more intimate act of love. Mouths still fused, she twisted and turned in his lap, and he helped her, guiding her with his hands until she faced him and her legs straddled his hips. By then, they were both breathing hard, and Grey was about to split the zipper on his shorts.

They both knew what was going to happen, but that only heightened their excitement. Hastily he shoved the straps of her negligee down her arms until the bodice bunched around her waist, leaving her gloriously bare for his pleasure. As he watched, her breasts swelled and grew taut. Leaning forward, he dragged his tongue over a budding nipple, then suckled her breast until she cried out, her fingers gripping his shoulders.

Finally he pulled back, letting his hands finish where his mouth had left off. "So, I guess I oughta show you just how much I love you, huh?" he teased, giving her the same sweet dose of medicine she'd given him the night they'd gone to dinner. The night he realized he was in love.

She arched shamelessly into the palms cupping her breasts. "Yeah, maybe you should," she said as she went to work tugging his shirt from the waistband of his shorts.

He was certain she could feel the wild beating of his heart against his chest. A heart brimming with so much feeling and emotion it was near to bursting. "Just in case you might have some doubts," he added, toeing off his shoes.

Her eyes sparkled with humor and love. "Yeah, just in case," she agreed.

Once he'd pulled his shirt over his head and tossed it aside, he reached between them, unbuckled his belt and

released his zipper. Leaning back in his chair while she shifted her weight, he pushed both his shorts and briefs down his thighs and kicked off the restraining garments.

There was so much more he wanted to do to her, but the need to be inside her obliterated everything else. Sliding his hands inside that strategic slit in the gown, he gripped the backs of her thighs and pulled her forward the same time he thrust his hips upward. The smooth tip of his erection glided through slick folds of flesh and found its home deep, deep within her body. She arched into him with a sharp, breathless cry. Groaning roughly, he buried his face in the fragrant curve of her neck and grazed his teeth along her throat.

He let her set the rhythm of their mating, enthralled by the wanton way she took her pleasure from him. His lips and tongue paid homage to her breasts, while his hands stroked her belly, her quivering thighs and eventually where they joined. His thumb circled and rubbed, and he whispered words of encouragement, and then more explicit demands her body had no defense against.

She came apart for him on a convulsive shudder and a whimper that echoed in his soul. Capturing her mouth with his, he moaned as his own climax ripped through him, hotter than fire and sweeter than the promise of heaven.

Love, he decided, made all the difference in the world.

Mariah wrapped her arms around his neck and sank drowsily against him, heartbeat to heartbeat. Their bodies were damp, their breathing labored. After a few minutes of rest she whispered against his throat, "Tell me again, Grey."

Shutting his eyes, he swept his hand down her back, savoring the flood of feelings only she evoked in him. "Oh, God, Mariah. I do love you."

He felt her smile against his shoulder. "I knew you did."

"WOMAN, YOU'RE GONNA kill me," Grey muttered as he lay on top of Mariah, still inside her, in the aftermath of their lovemaking. He felt totally satiated and downright exhausted after she'd taken advantage of his body. Again.

He'd carried her from the kitchen to the bedroom after the first time they'd made love, and she hadn't given him much time to recuperate before she'd shimmied out of that scrap of nothing and pulled him to her with a renewed vigor he couldn't help but respond to.

"At least you'll die a happy man," she said, skimming her palms down his muscled back to his buttocks.

Deep laughter rumbled in his chest. "Yeah, what a way to go." He groaned in her ear as she tensed inner muscles around him, then he lifted his head to look at her. "Lord, where did you learn to do that?"

"Jade loaned me some interesting books of hers." A sly smile curved her well-kissed mouth. The soft glow from the bedside lamp emphasized the mischievous gleam in her eyes. "I wouldn't want you to get bored with the predictable stuff."

Not in a million years, he thought. Separating their bodies, he lay back on the bed and gathered her close to his side, reveling in the simple pleasure of just holding her. "With you, making love has never been, and never will be, predictable."

Draping herself along his upper body, she stacked her hands on his chest and propped her chin on top. "Yeah, well, you've pulled a few unpredictable stunts of your own lately."

"Like?"

"All those flowers and sexy lingerie you sent me when we first broke up."

Plucking the pins from the knot of hair on her head, he plowed all ten fingers through the mass of silk. "Someone told me that women like to be romanced."

She rolled her eyes, then groaned when he stroked and massaged the warm nape of her neck. "Mark, no doubt, womanizer that he is."

He grinned wolfishly. "Yeah, but I have to admit his idea worked."

Closing her eyes, she relaxed as his hands moved to rub the muscles along her shoulders and the slope of her back. "Umm, it was kinda nice being spoiled like that," she admitted, a dreamy quality to her voice. "And what about kidnapping me?"

"Sheer desperation. And that worked, too."

"Only because I felt sorry for you."

He frowned. "What do you mean?"

Her sigh fluttered the light sprinkling of hair on his chest. She blinked her lashes open. "If I really wanted to find a way home I would have. I wanted to be with you, and I'm *soo* glad I came."

"Yeah, me, too." His finger traced the notches in her spine, and she arched against him like a sleek cat.

"I have to say, though, that this is the most unpredictable stunt you've pulled so far."

"What stunt is that?" he murmured suggestively. "The one in the chair, or the one at the foot of the bed when I pulled your legs around my—"

She gave him a playful pinch in the side, and he yelped. "I'm talking about the ring, Grey."

"Oh, the ring." Smiling, he smoothed a strand of hair behind her ear, keeping his gaze on hers. "I guess that's the kind of irrational thing you do when you're in love. Of

course, I can only assume my spontaneous behavior is related to love since I've never been in love before you."

"I'm glad I'm your first," she said in a seductive tone, and lightly rolled his nipple between her fingers.

"Yeah, me, too." He sucked in a breath as her fingers fluttered along his rib cage. "It's sorta like being a virgin all over again."

She arched a blond brow and drew sensual circles around his navel, then explored lower. "Now there's a fantasy I'd be happy to fulfill for you. Older, more experienced woman tutoring younger virgin boy." Her fingers wrapped around his semierect shaft, which thickened with each of her slow, measured strokes.

He moaned at the images her words projected in his mind, and grasped her hand to stop the sweet torture. "Give me ten more minutes for my poor body to recuperate from our first two *stunts*, and then I'll be happy to let you show me just how experienced you are."

Mariah pressed a kiss on his chest then snuggled into his side. They had the rest of their lives to indulge in fantasies. For now, she was content to bask in the triumph of Grey's declaration of love and the ring he'd put on her finger.

Lifting her left hand, she admired the band of sparkling rubies and diamonds, and the marquis set in the center of the exquisite, original design. It wasn't a traditional wedding ring by today's standards, but then Grey wasn't the traditional sort.

A grin tipped her mouth, and a giddy feeling tickled her belly. Her parents were going to be thrilled about her engagement to Grey. No doubt her mother would be anxious to help her plan the wedding, and her father wouldn't spare any expense on the grand event to finally see one of his daughters married.

She glanced up at Grey. His eyes were closed, but the fingers brushing along the curve of her waist told her he was awake. She supposed she ought to see if he had a preference for a particular date to exchange vows before they told her parents the good news.

"So, when do you want to get married, Grey?" she asked, unable to contain the excitement working its way to the surface. "I've always wanted a winter wedding, but I wouldn't mind getting married in the spring. Which do you prefer?"

The sudden tension in his body was nearly tangible. The fingers stroking her skin stilled, and his eyes slowly opened and met hers, dark and remote.

"Mariah, I never said anything about marriage." His voice was deceptively calm, though the muscle ticking in his jaw belied his tension.

Dread churned in the pit of her stomach, and she tamped down the knot working its way up her throat. This had to be an awful nightmare, but the pricking heat along her nerves confirmed she was wide-awake. Had she somehow misunderstood Grey's intentions? "But you said you loved me," she whispered, hearing the confusion in her own voice.

His heart thundered violently beneath the palm she rested on his chest. "I *do* love you," he said gruffly.

She shook her head, not comprehending how he could love her, offer her a ring, but stop short of fulfilling that commitment. "And the ring?"

He pulled his arm from around her, withdrawing physically as well as emotionally, and sat up on the edge of the bed, his back to her. "It's not a bridal set," he pointed out tightly. "I made sure of that."

She shivered, and grabbed for the quilt. She felt cold. The kind of chill that settled deep and clung to your

bones. "A 'bridal set' is anything you deem it to be," she said, swallowing back burning tears. "I'd proudly wear a ring from a Cracker Jack box to be your wife, Grey. If this ring you gave me isn't meant to be a wedding ring, then what would you call it?"

He wouldn't look at her. Silence filled the room, and the longer it stretched between them, the angrier Mariah became. She wanted to hit him, hard. Wanted to rail at him for making her believe that they could have a secure future together. Their relationship had seemed so hopeful after their week together. *She'd* been hopeful.

And so very wrong.

Her nerves snapped. "Dammit, Grey, answer me. You owe me at least that much."

His head whirled around and he glared at her, but there was pain in his gaze, too. And fear. "Why are you making this more complicated than it has to be?"

She lifted her chin, unwilling to back down on what she believed in. Marriage. A forever kind of commitment. Them. "Answer me. Why did you give me this ring?"

"It's the ultimate expression of how I feel about you." He hesitated. When she didn't respond, just waited for more of an answer, he took a deep breath and continued. "I love you. Right now, at this moment, I can't imagine anyone else in my life—"

"But that's subject to change?" she interrupted bitterly.

"Yes, I mean, *no!*" He jumped up and rounded the bed with a fierce curse. Grabbing the first thing he found, his sweatpants, he yanked them on. "Dammit, Mariah, that's not what I said. Quit putting words in my mouth," he said heatedly. "You know how I feel about marriage, and that hasn't changed. I doubt it ever will."

A strangled sound escaped her. *Oh, God.* Her heart was breaking, and she feared it would never mend. A horri-

fying sense of déjà vu wrapped around her. They'd had a similar conversation a few months ago when he'd asked her to live with him.

Despite all her efforts the past week, nothing had changed. *Grey* hadn't changed.

Get up and walk out, her mind urged, but her heart demanded more answers. Numbly, she slipped from the bed and started putting on the clothes she'd left out to wear home tomorrow. "What makes you think *my* feelings about marriage have changed?"

A deep frown creased his brows. "I thought we'd come to an understanding about our relationship."

Her brittle laughter masked the devastation tearing her apart inside. Apparently they'd come to vastly different conclusions about where their relationship was heading and where it would end. "Funny, I thought you knew I wouldn't settle for less than marriage." She'd believed they were working toward a common goal—to spend the rest of their lives together.

"And after everything I shared with you, about my parents, my mother and my childhood, I thought you understood my views on marriage." He dragged his fingers roughly through his hair. "I *never* led you to believe differently."

Her mouth opened, then snapped shut. He was absolutely right. The only comment she could use to refute his point was that she'd hoped she could show him how good a relationship could be between a husband and wife, and change his mind. Apparently he didn't care how wonderful a marriage could be.

She buttoned the front of her light cotton dress, realizing in that moment that they'd both secretly hoped to sway the other to their way of thinking. And when it came

right down to it, neither of them was willing to surrender their beliefs for the other.

"I guess I'd hoped you'd see how special what we have is," she said, her voice quiet.

"I do see how special what we have is," he said impatiently.

"But it's not special enough for you to marry me."

His jaw clenched hard. "I never said that."

"Not in so many words, but you might as well have, because that's what this discussion comes down to." She pulled in a big breath of air, needing the oxygen to go on. "You want me to wear your ring, but you don't want any of the responsibilities or the ultimate commitment that goes with it."

He turned away, walking to the window that faced the lake, which shimmered with the reflection of the rising moon. "I knew buying you that ring wasn't a good idea," he muttered in disgust.

"Then why did you?" she asked boldly.

"I told you why." He glanced over his shoulder, pinning her with his gaze. "I love you, Mariah."

Why isn't that enough? The unspoken question hung between them. *Because I want a husband who will cherish me, and I want children to love. I want one special man to spend the rest of my life with, not the insecurity of wondering when the magic was going to end—and be left with nothing more than the ashes of memories. I want to make memories, and pass them on to our family.*

But she didn't think Grey would understand her dreams. "So, essentially, you want me to live with you, sleep in your bed, wash your underwear and wear a ring that tells any man who looks at my ring finger that I'm taken, but at any given moment you could decide that

you're no longer in love and that living with a woman cramps your style?"

Irritation flashed in his gaze. "You make it sound like some kind of impersonal arrangement."

"It might as well be." She twisted the ring off her finger, feeling like she was physically severing herself from him, and set it on the nightstand next to his wallet. "This ring means nothing."

He looked from the ruby-and-diamond band to her, trying his best to conceal his hurt expression, and failing. "It means *everything* to me."

Unfortunately, their "everythings" differed dramatically. "Not to me. Not without marriage."

"I have no intention of getting married. Ever," he said succinctly, and not without a little hostility. "Why can't we just enjoy what we have for as long as it lasts?"

"Because I want it to last forever."

He sliced a hand impatiently through the air. "A piece of paper declaring us husband and wife hardly guarantees happily ever after."

"No, it doesn't. It's up to you and I to work together to make our life happy." She came around the bed toward him. Ludicrous as it seemed, she wanted to be near him for what precious moments were left of their unraveling relationship. "There are no guarantees in life, Grey. Maybe we'll divorce or, God forbid, maybe one of us will die tomorrow."

"And there's no guarantee that love will last," he argued.

"You're absolutely right." She stood in front of him, resisting the impulse to reach out and touch his tense body. "I know you've seen the worst of marriages and relationships, but I've seen some of the best. You can't let the horrible way your father treated you and your mother's

obsession about being loved influence your life and the chance to be happy with one special woman."

He said nothing, just stared at her, his eyes darkening with a despair that made her heart ache.

"People stay in love, Grey, as long as the couple continually works at it," she went on, a desperate part of her hoping she still had a chance in heaven of influencing him. "Love is fragile. For it to grow, it has to be nurtured and never taken for granted. People grow apart and divorce because they stop caring about each other, their family and the commitment they've made."

A mocking smile curled the corner of his mouth. "What makes you so sure that won't happen to us?"

His cynicism cut deeply. "I'm *not* sure, but as long as we communicate and respect one another, I think we could be really good together. You're my best friend, and I'd do whatever I could to make you happy."

"And I want to make *you* happy. I just don't think we need marriage for that." His voice rose in frustration. "Why complicate things?"

"Because I don't want to have children out of wedlock." The words tumbled out of her mouth faster than she could rescind them. But they were the truth, and it was an issue that needed to be discussed.

He blanched. "I never said anything about children."

She crossed her arms over her chest. "Except that you don't want them."

His mouth thinned into a grim line. "At least I'm honest about it. Kids need a father who can be there for them emotionally, who can raise them with a gentle but firm touch. I can't do that, Mariah. I don't know *how* to do that. All I know is the anger and cruelty I learned at my father's knee. I refuse to subject a child to that kind of ugliness."

He turned around and focused his attention some-

where out the window. Very quietly, very defeatedly, he said, "They'd be better off without me as a father."

A crushing pressure filled her chest, making it difficult for her to breathe. "You are so very wrong," she whispered. "They'd be very fortunate to have you as a dad."

He whirled around and scowled. "How the hell would you know?"

"From what you've told me about Aaron Nichols, I know firsthand you're a better man than your father ever was."

His laugh was self-depreciating. "I could be worse. Much worse."

She shook her head, refusing to be baited. "I wouldn't consider marrying a man who wasn't gentle and kind and loving. You have those qualities, Grey. And those qualities are what I love the most about *my* father."

She watched him struggle with some internal battle—wanting to believe her but allowing that vulnerable little boy in him to cling to the past and all the troubling memories of his childhood: the verbal abuse from his father and his mother's neglect.

Until Grey resolved those fears and insecurities, she knew they had no chance at a future.

He scrubbed his hand along his jaw, misery clouding his features. "So, what this all boils down to is you want all or nothing."

"Yeah, I guess I do. I'm afraid being someone's mistress isn't my style." She drew a deep shuddering breath, and although her heart felt torn and ragged, a strange calm swept over her. "I want to be your wife, Grey, and I want to be the mother of your children, not just the woman you happen to be living with and sleeping with. If you love me the way you say you do, then marriage would be the next

logical step in our relationship. Anything else we can work on together, as husband and wife."

He uttered a strangled sound, and his hands fisted at his sides. "Dammit, Mariah... I can't."

She couldn't stop the tears that stung the back of her eyes and spilled forward. "And I can't keep loving you and being with you day after day, not without a promise for a future together."

His own eyes misted, and his throat worked spasmodically. He took a step toward her, then stopped. "Mariah, please don't do this to us."

"I have no choice." Bridging the distance between them, she brushed her lips across his, wanting to forever remember the taste of him. His body shuddered in response, but he showed greater restraint than she and kept his hands to himself.

"I love you, Grey," she said softly, touching his cheek, his jaw, imprinting everything about him into her mind before letting her hand fall away. "I probably always will. Even if you don't realize it, you would have made a wonderful husband and a great father. One of these days you're going to realize exactly what you threw away, but by then it'll be too late. You'll be alone and lonely, wishing you had a wife to keep you company and grandchildren to spoil. Maybe, if you're lucky, one day you'll take a chance and find happiness with another woman."

"I don't want any other woman."

She smiled sadly. "And I don't want any other man, but I want a husband as well as a lover. Someone I know will be there for me when I'm old and gray and a little slow getting around. I want to come home to the same man for fifty years and still feel that surge of excitement I do every time I look at you. I want children to enrich my and my husband's life, and when they're grown, I want a man

who will still be my best friend, my lover, my life." A tear trickled down her cheek, but she didn't bother wiping it away. "I wanted that with you, Grey."

His anguish was real, so real she had to fight the urge to tell him to forget everything she'd just said, that she'd take him on any terms he demanded.

A thread of common sense kept her grounded to reality.

She swallowed the huge knot of sorrow lodged in her throat. She knew what she had to do, though she might have just as well carved her heart out of her chest while she was at it. "It's over, Grey, for good this time," she said in a choked voice, hating the words that would forever sever him from her life.

"Mariah, you can't mean this."

His despair ripped at her soul. "I do," she whispered, and turned to finish packing the bags. "The honeymoon is over, Grey, it's time to take me home."

10

MARIAH BLINKED HER EYES open and groaned. She wanted to die. From heartbreak. And from the miserable bout of flu that had lingered for the past week. The two combined was enough to give new meaning to the word *anguish*.

She glanced at the clock on her nightstand, unable to believe she'd slept until noon. She was so tired lately that no amount of sleep seemed to make her feel refreshed. With effort, she got out of bed, put on her old, favorite chenille robe and shuffled into the kitchen.

It was Sunday, but Jade wasn't home. Mariah was grateful for small favors. For the past five weeks since her second breakup with Grey, her sister had been doing her best to snap her out of her gloom, that is after Jade's initial "I told you so." But Mariah couldn't seem to summon up enough energy, or enthusiasm, to give in to her sister's prodding to "get on with her life."

Opening the freezer, she reached for a bowl of frozen grapes, then stopped when her stomach rebelled at the thought of any kind of food, even her favorite snack. Tears welled in her eyes and caught in her throat.

Damn. Now she was crying over frozen grapes. She'd been so emotional lately, the slightest, silliest things seemed to set her off and make her bawl like a baby. Jade was becoming impatient trying to gauge her mood shifts, not that she could blame her sister. *She* couldn't even anticipate her emotional state from one moment to the next.

Closing the freezer, she made her way to the kitchen table, sank into a chair and rested her cheek on the cool, wooden surface. She closed her eyes and attempted to relax and get a grip on reality.

The first two weeks back from the cabin she'd spent refusing Grey's calls at the office, listening to his pleas on her answering machine at home and making Jade turn him away at their door.

Then it all stopped. And the silence hurt worse than hearing the torment in his voice when he'd left his final "I love you" on her answering machine. She'd listened to it a zillion times since.

Mariah gulped back more tears. She missed him so much, and not for the first time wished they could go back to the cabin and the gentle, tender moments they'd shared, the fun, the laughter and the fierce loving that would haunt her forever. That one week had been romantic and idyllic. She'd hoped, and dreamed, and let herself believe that her love could change Grey. But in the end, her love, *their* love, hadn't been powerful enough to allow Grey to let go of his disturbing past and chance a future with her.

Sighing, she let her mind drift and the tension ease from her body. She grew lethargic. She was tired, so tired....

A hand settled on her shoulder and shook gently. "Hey, Riah, you okay?"

Mariah woke with a start and lifted her head from the table to find her sister standing beside her with a concerned expression on her face. "I'm fine," she said, her voice hoarse. Pushing her disheveled hair from her face, she glanced at the kitchen clock, which told her she'd been sleeping for nearly an hour. "I guess I just kinda drifted off."

"Yeah, well, you seem to be doing a lot of that lately,"

Jade said. "At your desk at work, in the bathtub, sitting on the couch and now at the kitchen table. At first I took it personally when you'd drift off while I was talking to you, as if I was boring you or something." She gave Mariah a critical once-over that made her uncomfortable. "And don't you think it's odd that you can't shake this flu you've had for the past week, and that I haven't caught it?"

Mariah frowned. "I haven't really given it much thought."

"Obviously," Jade said dryly as she plunked a small brown bag in front of Mariah. "But I have, and I think I finally figured out what your problem is."

Mariah had a feeling the cure was in the bag, which she eyed hesitantly. "What's this?"

"A little present for you." Jade sat in the chair next to hers. "Go on and open it."

Very tentatively, she did, and gasped when she saw the contents. "A pregnancy test? I'm sick, not pregnant!"

A brunette brow rose, enhancing Jade's dubious expression.

"I can't be pregnant," she said reasonably, even as she frantically counted back to the day of her last period, which had been light and only two days long, nothing like her normal five-day flow. Around the thundering of her heart, she managed, "I'm on the Pill."

"Which is only ninety-nine percent effective," Jade pointed out. "Humor me, Riah, and take the test."

Mariah stood, her stomach churning with a sudden dread she refused to acknowledge. "You're wrong," she said. Grabbing the little brown bag, she disappeared into the bathroom, praying that Jade was, indeed, mistaken.

Less than ten minutes later she walked back into the

kitchen, stunned to the point of numbness. Holding the test strip in her hand, she met Jade's anxious gaze.

"It's positive," she said, then burst into tears.

"Oh, Riah." Jade stood and wrapped her in a comforting embrace. She soothed her for a few moments, then took her by the hand and led her into the living room.

They sat side by side on the couch. "It's not as if I didn't try and warn you," Jade teased, trying to lighten the moment. "Nooo, now look at you, heartbroken *and* pregnant."

Mariah swiped away the wetness from her cheeks, her shock fading into disbelief. "I just don't understand how it happened."

Jade's mouth curled into a sly grin. "It happens when two people have that recreational activity called sex, not that I'd recall what that's like. It's been so long I can almost qualify as a born-again virgin."

Despite her situation, Mariah smiled. Staring at the bright blue plus sign on the strip confirming her delicate condition, she shook her head. "I guess I've just become a statistic."

Jade agreed, and after a few reflective minutes she asked, "What are you going to do, Riah?"

"I'm keeping the baby, of course," she said without a second thought. That wasn't an issue for her. Raising a child alone wouldn't be easy, and it certainly wasn't what she'd envisioned for herself, but she wouldn't consider any other option.

"I didn't doubt that you would keep the baby." Compassion softened Jade's features. "What I meant was, are you going to tell Grey?"

Mariah rested her head on the back of the sofa and stared up at the ceiling fan. The whitewashed oak blades whirled, casting blessedly cool air downward. A rush of

tears filled her eyes before she could stop them. Now she knew why she'd been on such an emotional roller coaster lately, and why the mere mention of Grey had her blubbering like a two-year-old.

But her tears changed nothing, especially the fact that Grey didn't want a family.

Swiping at the moisture trickling from the corner of her eye, Mariah drew a steadying breath and looked at Jade, her decision made. "No, I'm not telling Grey."

"Why not?" she asked gently.

For all her brashness, Jade could be so sensitive at times. Usually the right times. "I don't want Grey to feel obligated to a child he made clear he doesn't want."

Jade digested that, then countered with, "Don't you think he has the right to at least know about the baby?"

She shook her head emphatically. "If Grey knew, he'd feel responsible to marry me, and I refuse to force him to do something he doesn't want to." Just like Grey's mother and father. No way was she going to let Grey's history repeat itself with them. "He had his chance to marry me, and instead he let me walk away."

"You being pregnant might change his mind."

"For all the wrong reasons," she refuted. "He made his feelings on marriage and children very clear. I don't want to be an obligation to Grey, and this baby to be an unwanted burden, one he grows to resent. This isn't an issue that's up for negotiation."

Jade's cobalt blue eyes held understanding. "Well, you don't have much choice but to tell Mom and Dad about this new addition to the family. Not to mention the fact that you won't be marrying the baby's father."

Mariah's temples began to throb at the thought of breaking the news to her very old-fashioned father. Oh, he was going to be thrilled that he was finally going to be

a grandpa, and not so happy to learn she was going to be a single mom. "Mom and Dad will learn to adjust. This is the nineties. Women have babies on their own all the time."

They grew quiet, as if Jade sensed there was nothing she could say or do to change Mariah's mind.

And there wasn't.

Slipping her hand inside her robe, Mariah pressed her palm to her still-flat stomach, awed that a little life was growing inside her. There wasn't any doubt that the baby had been conceived at the cabin, and wondered if it had happened the night in front of the fire or the night Grey had told her he loved her.

The night her world had fallen apart.

This baby hadn't been planned by any means, but it had been created out of love. And her child would know love, Mariah thought determinedly. Lots of it. From a caring mom, a neurotic aunt and enthusiastic grandparents.

"Wow, a baby." Jade sighed, a wistful quality to her voice. "Do you think it's a boy or a girl?"

Mariah closed her eyes, envisioning a little girl with Grey's dark hair and golden eyes, then a little boy with similar coloring. "It doesn't matter, as long as it's healthy."

Jade grinned. "If my vote counts for anything, I hope it's a girl."

Mariah groaned, imagining the bond Jade would form with her niece. "And the first words out of her mouth would be, 'Let's go shopping.'"

"Of course." Jade laughed, her eyes sparkling wickedly. "Whatever it is, a boy or a girl, I plan to spoil this baby rotten."

Mariah wasn't sure she liked the sound of that. "Do I have any say in the matter?"

"Absolutely not." Jade's humor faded into a tender expression. "I still can't believe I'm going to be an aunt."

Grasping her sister's hand, Mariah gave it a reassuring squeeze. "You'll be the best."

"And you're going to be a mom." Her voice was filled with wonder.

Mariah rubbed her belly, already experiencing a fierce protectiveness toward her unborn child. "Yeah, though this isn't the way I'd planned it."

"Some things are better not planned."

Emotion constricted Mariah's throat. "Maybe you're right," she whispered.

"Aren't I always?" she said with her regular dose of sass. Then she grew serious. "I'll be here for you, Mariah, in any way I can."

Mariah reached over and gave her sister a warm hug. Damn. More tears. Would they ever stop? "Thanks, Jade, that means more to me than you'll ever know."

Jade pulled back, frowning. "Hey, what's with all the tears?"

"Damn hormones," Mariah muttered, though she knew hormones had little to do with it. These tears were for Grey and all the joy he was going to miss not being a part of his child's life.

"WASN'T THAT INCREDIBLE?" Mariah was still filled with excitement as she and Jade exited her obstetrician's office and walked across the parking lot to her car. She'd just had her five-month checkup and ultrasound, and was thrilled and relieved to find out the baby was healthy.

"Yeah, it was," Jade agreed, smiling. "It's amazing to hear that little heart beat and see the baby actually moving inside you." She gazed at the ultrasound picture the doctor had given Mariah, an X ray that outlined the

baby's head and body. In this particular pose, the baby was sucking its thumb. "Too bad the little critter wouldn't open up its legs so we could get a peek."

"Just think what a surprise it'll be when the baby is born." Mariah dug her car keys from her purse. "And you'll be right there in the delivery room when it happens."

"I don't know about this coaching stuff," Jade said as they slipped into the car. "You know the sight of blood makes me queasy."

"You'll be fine." Mariah buckled her seat belt over her rounded, ever-expanding waistline and gave her sister a reassuring pat on the knee. "I'll be the one in pain."

"Grey should have been here today, not me," Jade said quietly.

Mariah sighed, staring out the windshield at nothing in particular. She'd thought the same thing. When she'd seen and felt the baby move within her body she'd been breathless with wonder, and on the heels of that came a twinge of sadness that wrapped around her heart and squeezed tight.

She couldn't help but feel doubts and sometimes guilt for keeping Grey's baby a secret. He was the father of this baby, but her arguments always whittled down to one plain and simple issue. Grey didn't want children. Ever. Oh, she didn't doubt he'd take responsibility for the baby, but she didn't want his acceptance to be one of financial obligation. She wanted it to be borne of unconditional love for the child.

There was no question in her mind that he'd make a good, caring father. She'd told him as much. But the awful, bitter memories of Grey's father's abuse shadowed his confidence. And there was no way she could prove him wrong, not until he was ready to believe in himself, and in

his strength and ability to be a better man than his father was. She seriously doubted anything had happened in the past five months to change his way of thinking.

Wrapping her fingers around the steering wheel, she waited for the tightness in her chest to ease. Although the emotional ups and downs had subsided over the months, along with the morning sickness, there wasn't a day that went by that she didn't think about Grey. She was desperately trying to put him and their relationship behind her and focus on her future with their child. But forgetting Grey was impossible. Whenever she looked in the mirror and saw the changes to her body, she thought of the man who'd helped create the baby inside her. And she remembered the love they'd shared for one perfect week.

Finally she glanced at Jade. Her sister expected a response to her statement, she could tell, but she wasn't up to defending her decision. She did that often enough with her father, though her parents had come to accept her choice.

"I've got a craving for a Monte Cristo," she said instead, forcing a smile. "How about lunch on me at Maxine's?"

Jade lifted a dark brow. "That's way across town."

Mariah shrugged and started the car. "But it's my favorite place. I haven't been there since…" *Grey.* She swallowed the name always on her mind and forever in her heart and finished with, "Well, in a while. I've had a craving for a Monte Cristo for the past month."

Jade held her hands up in surrender. "Who am I to stand in the way of a pregnant woman's craving?"

Mariah grinned at her sister and lovingly patted her swollen belly. "You're a smart woman."

"Well, I DO HAVE TO SAY that your prices are more than fair, and your references are impeccable." Sam Haight set

Grey's five-page proposal back on the table and leaned back in the Naugahyde booth with a satisfied smile on his face. "I've put off a new security system long enough. The job is yours if you want it."

Grey stared at the older man for a moment, unable to drum up any excitement for the six-figure deal Sam Haight had accepted so effortlessly. The man hadn't quibbled on the high-tech security system Grey had recommended for his plush offices, and he hadn't tried dickering on the cost. Where was the elation that came from such an easy victory?

"Well, Grey, do we have a deal or not?" Sam asked. "I'm anxious to get the security system installed." He rubbed his hands together, as if this security system was a new toy and he couldn't wait to play with it.

He'd be crazy to turn down such an easy, profitable job. Grey motioned to their waitress to bring the check for their lunch, then turned back to Sam. "I'll have the contract drawn up and to you by the end of the week. Installation can start as soon as next Monday."

"Fabulous. I'm looking forward to doing business with you."

"I'm looking forward to doing the job." Grey's reply came automatically, considering he didn't look forward to doing much these days. Since his breakup with Mariah, work had become an escape, a way to keep his mind off what he'd let slip though his fingers. Even the ruthless drive he once had to build his security firm into a Fortune 500 company had lost its appeal and excitement.

One night, while sitting alone in the dark in his living room nursing a beer, he'd come to the realization that his life had no real purpose or direction. Oh, sure, he was wealthy enough that he could purchase anything money

could buy, but it wasn't material items he wanted. No, his longing went much deeper than purchasing something on a whim. The yearning had settled in his soul, making him feel restless, lonely and miserable.

Certainly the deep ache would fade in time, he kept telling himself. But, dammit, how long would he have to wait until his heart didn't hurt anymore? How long before he could look at another woman and not see something about her that reminded him of Mariah? How long before the deep regret of letting her walk out of his life would fade?

Forever. The thought was suffocating and scary.

The waitress arrived with the check, and Grey mentally shoved his disturbing thoughts back into the dark, secluded spot in his soul where he kept them hidden. After paying the bill, he grabbed his briefcase, and he and Sam slid from the booth, heading toward the entrance of Maxine's.

Grey passed a young, pretty hostess as she led a couple to a table, and she gave him a seductive smile that made her interest in him clear. He waited for a stirring of attraction, a spark of desire, but none came. He shook his head in frustration and anger. He'd become a goddamned monk since Mariah.

The waiting area was crowded with lunchtime patrons waiting for a table, forcing him to cut through the lounge. His steps slowed as his gaze slid over silky blond hair cut into a shoulder-length style that reminded him of Mariah's. He could have sworn he caught a whiff of the light floral fragrance she sometimes wore.

He shook his head. Hard. He couldn't see the woman's face, but then he already knew it wasn't her. It never was. One time he'd made a fool of himself in public, running after a woman who'd looked so much like Mariah from

behind, only to grab her arm, turn her around, and have the strange woman stare at him as if he was crazy.

Some days he thought he *was* losing his mind.

Keeping his eye on the neon Exit sign over the front doors of the establishment, he fumbled for the open roll of Tums in his slacks' pocket.

He heard husky laughter, so much like Mariah's. Grey swore beneath his breath as he crunched into a chalky tablet. Impatient to be gone from the restaurant and the memories that were beginning to crowd his mind, he pushed open the heavy carved doors, let Sam precede him, and started out behind him.

"Mariah Stevens, party of two, please," the hostess announced over the intercom.

Grey froze. His heart thundered in his ears, and his chest tightened painfully. He had to have misheard the page. Either that or he was closer to insanity than he'd originally thought.

"How long do I have to put up with these cravings of yours?" Grey heard a familiar voice ask from behind him. A sassy voice from the past.

That sweet laughter again. "Only four more months."

The woman groaned. "This I can handle, but I draw the line at pickles and ice cream."

The exchange seemed surreal to Grey, but he found himself slowly turning around. He let the door shut, rudely leaving Sam outside by himself. Grey couldn't bring himself to care, because this was probably some sort of dream anyway.

He saw the blonde and brunette heading toward the waiting hostess. Before he lost his nerve, he called, "Mariah?"

She turned around with a smile wreathing her beautiful face and her eyes bright with amusement, but when she

saw him, her whole expression changed into one of shock and disbelief.

Their gazes locked. "Grey?" Her voice cracked.

She clearly wasn't overjoyed to see him. She watched him warily and with an unreserved apprehension that annoyed him. Guests entered and exited the restaurant, but his sole focus remained on the one woman he couldn't forget.

Jade stepped in front of Mariah, her stance fierce and protective. "Grey, she doesn't want to see you, so I suggest you just leave and not make a scene."

Irritation propelled him forward, and he slowly wended his way around the people in the waiting area. He caught Mariah's gaze and held it. "Let me hear that from Mariah."

Jade's chin jutted out, but before she could respond, Sam came back through the doors. He glanced from Grey to Mariah, took in the scene that looked as though a showdown was about to happen, and said cautiously and with concern, "Uh, you two know one another?"

"Yes," Grey said the same time Mariah said, "No!"

"No?" He lifted a mocking brow, remaining focused on her face. *You've already forgotten how intimately we know one another?* his eyes asked. *You can put me out of your mind so easily when I've spent the past five months in pure misery, wanting no other woman but you?*

Eyes wide, she took a hesitant step back, but there was really nowhere for her to escape, considering the exit was behind him. *It's over Grey. It's over!* her look frantically told him. But it was the undisguised fear in the depths that made him pause. His steps slowed as he neared, and it was then that he realized she looked...different.

Her face was fuller than he remembered, but no less beautiful. His gaze traveled lower, following the collar of

her pale pink blouse to the generous swell of breasts at least a size larger than engraved in his memory. The blouse flared slightly at the waist and settled against a rounded belly too firm to be excess fat.

She was undoubtedly pregnant.

The savage pain and jealousy that lanced through him was near unbearable. His heart hurt. His mind reeled. More confusing was the brief thought that he wished the child was his. He swore bluntly.

"If you two will excuse us," Grey said tightly, glancing from Sam to Jade and giving them a look sure to quell any argument. "I'd like to talk to Mariah *privately* for a few minutes."

Mariah gave Jade a look of sheer desperation, but her sister only said, "You need to tell him."

Tell him what? Grey wondered. That she'd found another man willing to give her everything he couldn't?

Sam, taking his cue from Jade, nodded and stepped her way. "What do you say I buy you a drink?"

Grinning wryly, Jade hooked her arm through the one Sam offered. "Yeah, I think I could use a peach daiquiri."

Grey could have used a drink, too, but instead he gave the impatiently waiting hostess a tight smile and asked her to hold Mariah's reservation.

The hostess returned to her post and called another party, leaving Mariah and Grey in the midst of patrons coming and going from the restaurant. The spot wasn't ideal for a private conversation, but at this point Grey wasn't going to be picky, and he didn't think Mariah would agree to someplace secluded.

Mariah nervously dragged her tongue across her bottom lip and shifted uncomfortably. Finally, she spoke. "How are you?"

"Just dandy," he drawled sarcastically. "And you?"

She looked everywhere but at him. "Fine."

Despite being torn up inside, he wanted to touch her so badly his fingers tingled. But she wasn't his to touch any longer. No, judging by her condition, she belonged to another man.

That thought put a bitter taste in his mouth. "I see you didn't waste much time starting a family. Who's the lucky guy? Richard?"

Her gaze jerked back to his. A flash of hurt entered her eyes, then she quickly glanced away again. "It doesn't matter, Grey," she said softly.

"It sure as hell does," he bit out. The hostess looked their way, and he tried keeping his temper, and his voice, at a reasonable level. "We've been split up for, what, a whole five months now and you've managed to find yourself a new husband—"

"It could have been you, Grey," she said in response.

His jaw tightened. Silently he admitted that's what galled him the most. The pure, undiluted regret he lived with every day. He hadn't been able to offer her what she wanted, but that selfish, aching part of him didn't want anyone else to have her, either.

"So, you just happened to fall in love with someone else?" That selfish part of him lashed out, wanting to hurt her as much as he hurt. Love, he was quickly learning, wasn't always a pretty emotion. "That's pretty damned convenient, wouldn't you say?"

Her face flushed and she suddenly looked every bit as furious as he was. And deeper, he saw the hurt. Curiously it gave him little satisfaction.

"I didn't fall in love with anyone else." Her voice was low and modulated.

He laughed, a mocking sound. "I guess that just goes to

show you that you don't always need love to get married, do you?"

"I'm not married," she snapped, then gasped in shock at her confession.

He blinked, and like a cold dose of reality, her words seeped through the haze of anger blinding him to all the obvious signs. His gaze narrowed, and he took a closer look at Mariah and the changes in her body. He knew little to nothing about pregnant women, but gut instinct gnawed at him. Apprehension and fear mingled, along with a greater emotion he couldn't put a name to.

She placed a possessive hand on her stomach, her expression reflecting her panic. "Grey, I have to go," she said abruptly, and turned toward the bar to retrieve her sister.

Without a thought he grabbed her arm, stalling her. His heart pounded so hard he could hear each drumming pulse in his ears.

She tugged on her arm, but his grasp was strong. "Let me go."

"Whose baby is it?" he asked, his voice as tight as the pressure banding his chest.

"Mine," she said fiercely.

He ground his teeth. "Dammit, Mariah, who is the father?"

"It's none of your business!"

He leaned close. "I'm making it my business!"

Tears filled her eyes and her bottom lip trembled. With great effort he resisted the urge to pull her into his arms, comfort her and apologize for his callous behavior.

He wasn't sorry. And he wanted answers. He didn't question why the need was so strong, only knew that he couldn't let her go without knowing the truth.

"Mariah," he said, his low voice vibrating with warning. "There are tests to prove paternity."

Dismay flitted across her face and shimmered in her gaze. "Why do you care?" she cried.

Because I love you. That's the only explanation his heart and mind would allow, and he didn't fight it. "Answer me," he said harshly.

She closed her eyes, and when they opened again he saw, as well as felt, her defeat. "You, Grey," she whispered in a choked voice as a single tear trickled down her cheek. "You're the baby's father."

Stunned, he let go of her arm and felt himself sway backward. He tried to drag a breath of air into his lungs, but oxygen suddenly seemed in short supply.

You, Grey. You're the baby's father. Her words reached him on some distant plane. He was going to be a dad. He gave his head a shake, and attempted to push aside the terror crashing over him. Oh, God, he couldn't be a dad. He didn't know how to be a dad. What if he failed? What if he was as rotten as his own father had been? The prospect was so frightening, so overwhelming in its capacity, that he felt ill.

Mariah pushed past him and out the door, snapping him out of his dark thoughts. He went after her, catching her halfway down the walkway leading to the parking lot. "Dammit, Mariah," he said, standing in front of her and forcing her to stop. "I'm not done talking to you!"

She lifted that stubborn chin of hers. Sunlight danced in her soft, silky hair and fire flashed in her eyes. "There's nothing to talk about."

He begged to differ. "Why didn't you tell me about the baby when you found out you were pregnant?" he asked with more calm than he felt.

"Because you were better off not knowing," she said bluntly.

He flinched as if she'd physically slapped him. What kind of monster did she think he was—to think he didn't care about her welfare? "Since I'm the father, I have a responsibility to that child."

"A responsibility you've made more than clear you don't want," she argued heatedly.

His jaw clenched in aggravation. "But mine nonetheless."

"I don't want or expect anything from you. I'm fully prepared to raise this child on my own." She laid a possessive hand over the swell of her belly, a protective instinct as old as time. "I don't want this baby to be some great, noble sacrifice for you. An *obligation*. I deserve better than that, and so does your child."

Her words felt like a double punch to the stomach. Oh, Lord, she was right. She *did* deserve better, so much better. And so did their child. The thought made his heart twist peculiarly. But the irrefutable truth was, the baby she carried was better off not having him as a father. He knew nothing but the worst about raising a child and being a dad, and he didn't think there was a sufficient manual on the how-to's of fatherhood for him, either.

A strange sense of despair wrapped around him. Fear clashed with regret, and added to the muddled mess was the deep longing of the confused, mistreated youth he'd been.

But he was a grown man, shaped by his childhood and educated through the school of hard knocks; his teacher a cruel, bitter man who'd taught his son humiliation and the worst kind of degradation.

He gulped in a breath. There was one last selfless act he could do for his child. It killed him to turn and walk away,

made a part of his soul shrivel and die, but he did just that.

There was no way he would ever subject a child to the kind of hell he'd been through.

11

GREY GLANCED at his watch as he cut through the courtyard located in the center of the Wilshire Plaza, and picked up his step. He was nearly half an hour late for the final fitting appointment with his tailor for the custommade suits he'd ordered.

His entire life had become a blur since seeing Mariah again. He went through the motions of work and everyday life, but his brain was in a fog, unable to remember something as simple as an appointment or a business meeting. Thank God he had Jeanie to prod his memory and keep him from totally sinking into the depths of his misery.

A baby. They were going to have a baby, or rather, according to Mariah, *she* was going to have the baby. On her own. Without his help or input. She'd made it clear that she neither expected, nor wanted, anything from him.

And so, without a fight, he'd walked away from Mariah and their child, and had spent every day since convincing himself he'd done the right thing. Both mother and child deserved better than what he could offer them, like emotional stability and a secure family environment filled with happiness and love. How could he give either when all he'd ever experienced was hostility, resentment and neglect? The fear of failing as a husband and father was always at the surface, rearing its ugly head, taunting him with powerful, ugly memories he had no defense against.

So why couldn't he shake the awful feeling that he was making the biggest mistake of his life?

Pushing that haunting question from his mind because he had no logical answer, he rounded a large fountain in the center of the courtyard and focused on the men's department store within sight.

He heard a whimper and a gulping sob, and automatically glanced around the area for the distraught sound while still keeping up his clipped pace. The courtyard was bordered with benches for weary shoppers to rest, and planter boxes with lush green foliage sectioned off individual alcoves. It was early afternoon on a weekday, and there was a sparse number of shoppers around the plaza. In fact, he didn't see anyone in the courtyard.

The pitiful whimpering sobs reached him again, the sound soft, but unmistakable. Frowning, he slowed his steps and glanced in the alcoves as he passed them. When he found the source of the distressing noise, he stopped, but made no move to advance toward the little girl huddled into the corner between the bench and planter box. When she saw him, she pulled her legs up to her chin and wrapped her arms around her knees. She watched him warily, fearfully, as silent tears streamed down her smooth cheeks.

She was a little thing, he thought, with honey brown hair that shimmered to her shoulders and big, watery blue eyes that grabbed at something deep inside him. Judging by her small size, he estimated her age between four and six.

She was obviously lost and scared. At the moment, he could relate. It was akin to how he felt—out of his element and antsy to be on his way.

But as uncomfortable as the situation made him feel, he

couldn't walk away and leave the little girl, hoping that whoever she belonged to eventually found her.

He took a tentative step toward the little girl. She shrank from him, her whole body trembling. Her whimpers increased, and his stomach twisted with dread. God, was he that threatening? He supposed to someone a third his size he'd seem like a giant. Or did children have a sixth sense about people who weren't adept with kids?

The thought was disturbing.

Shoving his hands into his slacks' pockets, he glanced around for help, but they were alone. Not a frantic mother in sight, or even a person of the female persuasion who'd know how to handle such a crisis. Since he couldn't leave the little girl alone, he was on his own. He grappled for the appropriate resources in dealing with a lost child, and his mind drew a blank.

"Are you okay, honey?" he asked in a soft, gentle tone. Stupid question, considering the girl was clearly distraught, but it was all he could think of as an icebreaker.

"I want my mom," she whimpered, her chin quivering.

He shifted casually, a subtle move that eased him closer. "Where is your mom?"

"I don't know." She sniffled, her expression bleak. "I only stopped at the toy store to look in the window, and when I looked back up, my mom wasn't there."

And most likely, the little girl's mother had eventually glanced down expecting to find her daughter by her side, and was met with the shocking discovery that her little girl was gone. No doubt, her mother was hysterical with worry.

The little girl started crying again, making Grey feel helpless and way out of his element. The first thought that drifted though his mind was, what would Mariah do? The answer came easily. She'd comfort the little girl.

Forcing himself closer, despite how the girl's sobs shook him up, he hunkered down in front of her. She was so little, so vulnerable. So sweet and innocent. Without thinking, he gently brushed a soft strand of hair from her face, startled by the odd protectiveness that rippled through him.

He swallowed hard. Oh, man, if he experienced such sensitivity and empathy with a child he didn't even know, he could only imagine how much more powerful the emotion would be with his own child.

His child. The child Mariah carried. The revelation sent his mind reeling.

"My name is Grey," he said, attempting to establish some familiarity between them and chase away her apprehension. "What's your name?"

"B-B-Brandi," she stuttered.

He smiled, the last of the tension easing from his body. "Well, that's a beautiful name for such a pretty little girl. What do you say you come with me and we'll go look for your mom?"

Her gaze turned skeptical, and she swiped her tears from her cheeks. "I'm not supposed to go anywhere with strangers."

"That's a very good rule," he told her, knowing he'd want his own child to be just as educated. "But I don't want to leave you here all by yourself. There's an information booth a little ways from here, and I'm sure they can locate your mom for you, but you have to come with me."

He straightened, held out his hand and waited, knowing there was little he could do if Brandi refused to go with him. If she didn't, he resolved to stay with her until someone found them.

Tentatively she reached out and placed her tiny, soft

hand in his much larger one, believing his promise. Believing and accepting *him*. That first touch and the way she curled her fingers so hopefully around his hand made his heart catch in his chest. Those big blue eyes, just moments ago brimming with tears, now shone with a trust that nearly brought him to his knees. She was depending on him to deliver her safely to her mother. There was no way he was going to let her down.

Adjusting his long stride to meet her much shorter one, he walked with her to the information booth and reported the incident to the young woman working there. The woman assured him that the little girl had been reported missing, and that security and the girl's mother were searching the plaza. Picking up a two-way radio, she called off the pursuit.

"They're at the other end of the plaza," the young woman said. "As soon as they locate Brandi's mother, they'll be here." She glanced over the counter at the little girl clinging to Grey's side. "Would you like to sit behind the counter with me until your mother gets here?"

Brandi shook her head and curled her fingers tight around Grey's hand. "No, I want to stay with Mr. Grey."

The woman glanced at Grey, and deciding he met with her approval, she smiled. "Very well."

Spotting an ice-cream shop across from the information booth, Grey glanced back at Brandi and said spontaneously, "What do you say we get an ice cream while we're waiting?"

A beatific smile wreathed the little girl's face, and she nodded eagerly. "I like chocolate," she announced.

Grey laughed. "Then chocolate it is."

Minutes later they were sitting side by side on a wooden bench next to the information booth, each holding a single-scoop chocolate ice-cream cone. The simplic-

ity of the situation seeped through him, warm as sunshine. He couldn't remember the last time he'd eaten an ice-cream cone, and that he was doing so with a child, and enjoying it bewildered and delighted him.

He was going to be a dad. The startling thought rushed out of nowhere, but it came with an abundance of emotion and a yearning he'd tried his best to ignore since learning Mariah was pregnant with their baby. A child conceived out of the love he and Mariah shared.

The longing for the impossible grew stronger with each passing day. Today it had surpassed anything he'd ever experienced, all because of a lost little girl. To help her, he'd played a role, a parental role he hadn't believed himself capable of. He'd been gentle and patient, despite his fears. And once they'd gotten over their initial wariness of one another, the rest had come naturally.

The prospect of raising a child made his insides clench with apprehension, but the thought of missing the opportunity to share in special moments like this with his son or daughter hurt much, much more. His own childhood had been less than ideal, full of painful memories that he'd never forget, that would always be a part of who he was. But as a result of what he'd experienced, he never, ever wanted his child to feel the kind of hurt and disillusionment he had. Never wanted his son or daughter to think he didn't love them.

And he *would* love them, he realized with startling clarity. Already did. He wanted to experience their smiles and laughter. To play ball with a son, or attend his daughter's ballet recital. Dammit, he wanted to be a part of their lives on a daily basis and share every stage of their development.

He wanted to make a difference to them, just as he'd

made a difference to this little girl who'd so openly trusted and accepted him.

You're a better man than your father ever was. You're kind, gentle and loving.... Mariah's words whispered through him, soothing the last of his doubts. She believed in him. She was strong, nothing even remotely close to his own weak, spineless mother. Mariah loved fully, without reservation, without conditions.

And she loved him. How could he fail with her by his side, guiding him and learning the ropes of parenthood right along with him?

He'd been a fool to walk away. What Mariah wanted was so simple, and something he'd yearned for his entire life, but had done his best to deny: to be part of a family, one filled with hopes and heartaches, good times and bad, respect and trust...and love.

He wanted it all. But would Mariah forgive him for being such an idiot and not realizing sooner that everything he'd ever wanted in his life started and ended with her?

Brandi patted his arm to get his attention, and he glanced from the chocolate handprint on his sleeve, to the little girl's face, smudged with sticky ice cream. He waited for a spark of irritation over the stain she'd left on his shirt, something to indicate he truly was his father's son and had a temper to match, but the only thought that came to mind was that his shirt was washable.

Pure relief flooded him, and at that moment, he knew he'd fight until his last breath for Mariah and his child.

"Thank you, Mr. Grey," Brandi said softly, gazing up at him with something akin to adoration. "You're very nice, and I like you a lot."

A lump the size of a baseball lodged in his throat, and he cleared it away before he embarrassed himself. "And you're the sweetest little girl I've ever had the pleasure to

meet." He tapped his finger on the tip of her nose, and when she giggled, he melted inside.

"Brandi!"

The frantic cry caught both Grey and Brandi's attention. When Brandi saw her mother running toward her, she scrambled off the bench and flew into her mother's arms.

The woman was crying and squeezing the little girl fiercely, protectively. "Thank you so much for taking care of my baby," she said, meeting Grey's gaze over her daughter's head. "One minute she was right next to me, and the next, she was gone. I've never been so scared in my entire life!"

Grey smiled, clearly picturing how he'd first found Brandi, crying and so frightened. "I think the feeling was mutual."

The reunion was sweet. And so were the strange but wonderful emotions sweeping through Grey. He knew he'd never see the little girl again, but he would never forget her.

"BUCKLE UP."

Mariah cast Grey an annoyed look, but did as he requested, considering he was already backing his Cherokee out of the parking spot next to her BMW. She never knew what to expect from him anymore, since the day he'd barged into her office two weeks ago demanding she allow him to be a part of his child's life. She couldn't help but wonder what had brought about the sudden change of mind.

She sighed, feeling impatient and weary. "Grey, you can't keep kidnapping me every time we get into an argument."

He slid on his sunglasses and merged into traffic. "I'm not kidnapping you."

"Then what do you call that stunt you pulled back in the parking lot? 'Get in the car and please don't make a scene,'" she said, reciting his exact words.

A grin curved his mouth. "Hey, I was polite about it. There were people around—I didn't want them listening to our conversation. Since you didn't argue and got into the car, I figured you felt the same way."

She ground her teeth at his logic. "Jade will be expecting me back at the office in an hour."

"Jade can wait. This can't." He stopped the car at a red light, and glanced at her. "We need to talk, Mariah."

She could only see her reflection in his glasses, but his intense gaze burned through the lenses like a laser. She'd been so emotional lately, she knew she'd bawl when that "talk" made her think about how hopeless and tangled their situation was.

"I don't want to talk," she said, her tone firm.

"Fine, then you can listen."

She didn't want to listen to what he had to say, either, but other than jumping from the vehicle, she had no choice. Determined not to say a word or contribute to this conversation in any way, she focused her attention out the passenger window.

He turned onto the freeway on-ramp. "You know I want to be a part of my child's life—"

Her head snapped around and she cut him off before he could complete his sentence. "I told you I wouldn't deny you that." So much for being quiet and unresponsive.

A small smile quirked the corner of his mouth. "Good, because I'm not giving you a choice."

She bristled in irritation. Who did he think he was that he could make ultimatums like that? *The baby's father, that's who.* He had every legal right to demand equal time with his child.

"I want to be a part of your pregnancy, too."

"You do?" she asked doubtfully and a little suspiciously.

"Yeah." Excitement laced his voice. "I can go with you to the doctor's appointments, can't I?"

"Yes." She nearly choked on the word, but knew she couldn't deny Grey the chance to hear the baby's heartbeat, and maybe see the baby move within her belly. She blew out an aching breath. Sharing the stages of her pregnancy with Grey was going to be joyful, as well as painful. She wondered if she'd survive this new unorthodox relationship they were establishing, one based on their mutual responsibility to the child inside her and nothing more.

"And how about those classes where they teach you to relax and breathe that funny way?"

"Lamaze." That's where she firmly drew the line. Lamaze was too personal and intimate an experience, one that required touching. How could she concentrate on her breathing technique in class when the man she loved but couldn't have was rubbing her back or gently caressing her belly? Her focus would be on *him*, not the lessons she needed to learn.

"Jade is going to be my coach," she said, hoping to dispel any notion or obligation he felt to be by her side during those laboring hours.

"No way," he said adamantly. "No offense to Jade, but I want to be there when the baby's born."

Feeling drained and uncertain about this whole part-time parent stuff, Mariah rested her head on the seat. "Grey, you don't have to do this—"

"I want to do this. I *insist* on doing this." He exited the freeway and came to a halt at the Stop sign at the base of the off-ramp. He transferred his gaze to her for a second

to give her the full effect of his grim expression. "You're not going to make my participation in this baby's life difficult, are you?"

She shivered in apprehension, wondering if he'd go so far as to sue for custody if he didn't get his way. "Of course not," she said, her temper rising. "I just don't want you to think that I'm going to make demands on your time."

He smiled very slowly, erasing that intimidating expression. "You won't have to, because I'm going to be around a lot."

Great, just great. She rubbed her forehead as the car rolled forward, moving onto surface streets. "I know you're busy, Grey. I don't expect you to see the baby every day—"

"I'll make the time. Every day."

Mariah took a deep calming intake of air. There was little she could say to his insistence on being a daily part of his child's life. She wanted that for this child, to know its father and spend time with him on a regular basis. But how was she going to survive seeing Grey every day, knowing that he had a life separate from hers—one that didn't include her, only their child?

He pulled into his driveway and cut the engine in front of his enormous, elegant two-story house. She stared up at the structure, a house built and designed for a bachelor with no intentions of getting tied down to a wife, and certainly not a child who would track dirt onto his light-colored carpet and leave toys strewn from one end of his impeccably clean house to the other. No, a family hadn't been in Grey's future thinking, and she worried how father and child would adjust when she wasn't there to smooth out the awkward moments between them.

The warmth of Grey's large hand beneath her blouse,

then sliding down the waistband of her stretch pants startled her out of her thoughts. Her breath caught sharply and she grasped his wrist, though he didn't seem inclined to remove his hand from the taut curve of her belly. Their gazes locked, his so full of wonder and awe she wanted to cry.

"Grey..." Her voice quivered, as did her body. She'd missed his touch, and hated that she was so weak she didn't have the will to pull his hand away.

His fingers probed her firm stomach. "I've been wanting to do this since the day at your office, but I was afraid you'd sock me one." He smiled ruefully.

Her grip on his wrist relaxed, foolishly giving him free rein to explore her stomach. "What makes you think I won't now?"

He chuckled, the deep, sexy sound making her shiver. "I'll take my chances, sweetheart," he said, his voice amused. "Have you felt the baby move?"

She smiled, wanting nothing more than to share her body's changes with Grey. "Yes."

His eyes sparkled enthusiastically. "What does it feel like?"

How could she explain such an indescribable sensation? "It feels like a butterfly fluttering around in my belly, with a few swift jabs for good measure." Without thinking of the implications, she slid her palm over the back of his hand and guided him lower, to the spot where their baby liked to fuss and kick about the most.

His gaze dropped to her heavy breasts, taking in the changes there while his fingers drew lazy circles on her belly. Gradually he dragged his gaze back up, stopping brief.y on her mouth, then onward to her eyes.

"You look beautiful like this, you know," he said huskily.

He was melting away her defenses by attacking her weak points—her desire and love for him. "Grey, don't do this—"

He cocked his head innocently, making him more irresistible than he already was. "Do what?"

Swallowing the thick need gathering in her throat, she withdrew his hand from beneath her blouse, which he allowed without protest. "Make this arrangement any more difficult than it already is."

"Is there something wrong with telling a woman she looks beautiful? Especially when that woman is carrying my child?"

Yes! she wanted to scream. Especially when this woman's heart had been shattered into a million pieces, and probably would never recover. Biting her lip to keep the words from escaping, she turned her gaze away from him.

With a gentle, persuasive pressure of his fingers on her chin, he brought her face back toward him again. "I haven't stopped wanting you, Mariah," he said, his voice soft and sincere. "If anything, the time we've been apart has only intensified my feelings toward you. Made me realize exactly what was missing from my life."

She pulled her chin from his grasp, trying not to soften to his will. It proved to be one of the most difficult feats of her life. "What are we doing here, Grey?" she asked tiredly.

He stared up at the house for a long, quiet moment, then said, "There's something I want to show you. Will you come with me?"

She opened her mouth to say no and request that he take her back to Casual Elegance. But there was something in his eyes, a combination of hope and anticipation that changed her answer to yes. At her nod, he released a

relieved breath, quickly climbed out of the car, and came around for her.

With her hand secured within his, she followed him inside the house and up the staircase to the second floor. All the while she sensed the coil of nervousness in his body with every step he took. He paused at the guest bedroom, his free hand resting on the doorknob.

Mariah frowned. What was so spectacular about his guest room that so obviously had him tied up in a knot of tension? He slowly opened the door...and then she knew.

Nothing had prepared her for what she saw or the overwhelming emotions tumbling through her. He released her hand, and as if drawn by invisible strings, she tentatively stepped inside the newly redecorated room.

A nursery. Oh, God.

A whitewashed crib, matching changing table and dresser replaced the queen-size canopied bed and armoire that had occupied the room before. A rocking chair was positioned near the window, a big, soft teddy bear with a huge red bow sitting in the seat.

Her chest tightened when she realized the wallpaper was the one she would have chosen—a carousel of plump, whimsical zoo animals shaded in soft pastel colors. Everything matched the design, from the crib set and border running along the top of the room, to the diaper holder and the curtains framing the window. Obviously the room had been professionally decorated, but how had Grey known this was the design she'd envisioned for her own nursery?

Despite herself and the pain slowly invading her body, she moved into the room and toward the crib. She touched one of the stuffed animals hanging from the mobile, and the attached music box tinkled out a strain of

"You Are My Sunshine." There was no doubt her baby would be happy here, in this delightfully decorated room.

A sob of despair broke from her. Tears blurred her vision, but she managed to blink them back. Dammit, this just wasn't fair!

"What, you don't like it?" At some point Grey had moved beside her. "Jade swore this was the pattern you said you wanted for the baby's nursery."

"Oh, it is." Damn Jade, anyway. How could her sister betray her this way?

"Well, then?" He clearly wanted an explanation for her emotional outburst.

She forced a smile, which was shaky at best considering she was dying inside. This part-time custody was going to kill her. "I'm sure the baby will love it."

He pushed his hands into his trouser pockets. "I'm hoping so, since he or she will be spending so much time here."

She stared at him in sudden horror. Had he gone through so much trouble with the nursery because he was considering full-time custody? The thought made her blood jell and her defenses rise. "You have every right to see this child as often as you'd like," she said in a voice that belied the fury steaming within her. "But I refuse to allow this baby to be raised by a nanny."

"A nanny?" An infuriatingly gentle smile touched his mouth and entered his eyes. "Oh, I must have forgotten to tell you—"

"Tell me what?" she demanded haughtily.

"That I want you to live here, too."

She tried, but failed to contain the hysterical laughter bubbling in her. "That's quite a convenient arrangement for you."

"Yeah, I guess it is." He shrugged nonchalantly. "But

then why wouldn't I want my baby and my wife living in my house?"

White-hot anger swirled within her, hazing his words. "You know how I feel about living with you, and I resent the fact that you'd use this baby to...to..." His comment slowly seeped through her tirade, and her heart nearly stopped. "What did you say?" she breathed, afraid to believe, to hope.

"I said—"

"But do you mean it?" she asked swiftly, as if Grey speaking the words out loud would somehow dilute their meaning.

"Yes, I—"

"You *really* want to get married?"

He separated the distance between them, wrapped one arm around her back and hauled her to him, using his free hand to cover her mouth. "Yeah, I *really* want to."

"Mrmph—"

"Hush, Mariah," he said gently. Then, as if knowing what assurances she was searching for, he went on. "I want to get married, not because I think it's the right thing to do, or even because of the baby. It's because I love you, and I'm miserable without you. I want to be that person you grow old with, the person who shares your hopes and dreams."

This time when she looked into his eyes she didn't see any of the doubts or fears that had plagued him for so long. No, he was finally free of past burdens, free to love and be loved. She didn't think it possible to feel so much joy.

Pulling his hand from her mouth, she smiled up at him. "You're pretty darn close to making all my dreams come true."

He folded her into his embrace and rubbed his cheek

against her hair, speaking near her ear. "I was so afraid of falling in love, but you know what? That fear doesn't compare to the fear of losing you. I know it won't be easy, being a husband and a father, but I'm going to do my damnedest to make sure you don't regret marrying me."

Mariah lifted her head to look up at him, content and secure in his arms. "How could I, when I've waited my whole life for you?"

He sank his fingers into her hair and tilted her face up to his for a tender kiss. He sighed against her lips, then grinned. "Thank God I came to my senses in time."

"Yeah, you were a little slow in coming around." She wound her arms around his neck, pressing herself against the muscular heat of his body. "Are you sure this is what you want? Marriage *and* a baby?"

His eyes gleamed like gold. "Absolutely, without any doubts."

She toyed with the collar of his shirt, needing a deeper explanation for Grey's change of heart. "What changed your mind?"

He told her about a lost little girl he'd found, and how that one incident had changed his entire outlook on his future, and his ability to be a good, caring father.

"I want to give my son or daughter everything I never had as a child," he continued, his voice deep with conviction, "unconditional love. My undivided attention. A father they can be proud of. I want to make a difference in my son or daughter's life. And your strength and love will help me along the way. I'll probably need as much guidance as our child, but I know I can do this with you at my side."

She smiled, realizing that he'd finally come to terms with his past—and wanted to make a better childhood for his own baby. "I'm with you every step of the way."

He brushed the back of his knuckles across her cheek, his gaze reverent. "I want us to be the family I never had, and the family you've always wanted."

"Oh, Grey," she whispered. This time, the tears that filled her eyes were of pure happiness. "I do love you."

"Yeah, I love you, too. And that's a guarantee you can count on," he murmured. He sealed his vow with a breath-stealing kiss that left no doubts in her mind, or her heart, that he was in this for the long haul.

_____Epilogue_____

"OKAY, MARIAH, when the next contraction comes I want you to push real hard, and that should do it," her doctor said from the opposite end of the laboring table.

"Come on, honey," Grey whispered encouragingly as he rubbed the spot low on her back he knew had been bothering her since her contractions had begun nearly ten hours ago. He was amazed what women endured during labor, and how strong and determined Mariah had been throughout the long, drawn-out process.

But now, after all her hard work, his continuous pacing and the application of what they'd learned together at her Lamaze class, they were nearing the end of what was turning out to be the most incredible experience of his life.

He took a deep breath, his insides clenching, not with fear, but anticipation. This baby had changed his life in so many ways, and he or she wasn't even born yet. The thought was staggering, because the rest of their lives lay ahead, with so many lessons to learn along the way, and so much love to give.

Mariah began her breathing, indicating another contraction was on its way. He tensed right along with his wife, and perspiration dotted his brow as well as her own.

"Come here, Dad, quick," the doctor said to Grey. "This is something you don't want to miss."

Grey was torn between obeying the doctors orders and remaining by his wife's side. Mariah made the decision

easy. With a reassuring smile, she said in between pants of breath, "Go, I'll be fine."

Grey rounded the table and stood next to the doctor, his eyes widening at the miracle in process. "Oh my God, the head's out!"

Mariah gave a strangled laugh that turned into groan as her belly spasmed. She gave a mighty heave as her body demanded, and Grey watched as their baby slipped into the doctor's capable hands. Wearily Mariah slumped back onto the bed.

The baby wailed. Grey stood stunned, awed, paralyzed by an overwhelming wave of emotions as he watched this tiny baby squirm in the doctor's hands.

"It's a girl," the doctor announced with a broad smile, and the nurses standing nearby issued verbal congratulations. Grabbing a pair of sterile scissors, he handed them to Grey. "The honor's all yours, Dad."

Grey stared at the scissors in horror, until the doctor chuckled and explained, "You get to cut the umbilical cord."

Nervously, Grey severed the connection between the baby and Mariah. Then the nurses quickly whisked the child away to be cleaned and have her vital statistics checked.

Still stunned, he made his way back to Mariah's side. "A daughter," he whispered, because he still didn't trust his voice not to crack. "We have a daughter."

Mariah smiled tiredly. "Yeah, we do."

Grey didn't think it possible, but his love for Mariah had increased over the past four months of their married life, had grown richer with each passing day. After the priceless gift she'd given him today, he was near bursting with emotion. "Thank you."

She grabbed his shirt and pulled him down for a quick kiss. "I think you had a hand in this, too, Nichols."

"A hand?" he murmured, grinning wickedly against her soft mouth. "I thought it was that other part of my anatomy that did the trick."

Mariah rolled her eyes, and he chuckled.

A few minutes later a nurse returned with their squalling daughter. To Grey's chagrin, she unceremoniously plopped her into his arms. Kayla, as he and Mariah had decided to call her, had a healthy pair of lungs and had no problem voicing her displeasure. Her face was beet red, and her little hands curled into angry, flailing fists.

Shaken by Kayla's distress, Grey looked to Mariah for help. He'd been poised and controlled all through the birth. Now he felt nervous and uncertain. His daughter depended on him, and he hadn't a clue as to how to soothe her.

"What do I do?" he asked anxiously.

Mariah gently touched the baby's head, stroking the soft, dark tuft of hair there. "You hold her close and you love her," she said simply.

As he cuddled his daughter securely and gently rocked her, Kayla's cries settled and she stared up at him, listening to his deep voice as he crooned to her. She was beautiful, he thought with pride as tears stung the backs of his eyes. He fitted his finger into her little palm, and his heart gave a funny tug as she latched on, trusting him, counting on him to be there for her. And he would be. Always.

In that instant, the precious bond between father and daughter formed. He lifted his gaze to Mariah and smiled, feeling like the luckiest man in the world.

Hold her close and love her. Grey didn't think that was going to be a problem. Not when she already had him wrapped around her little finger.

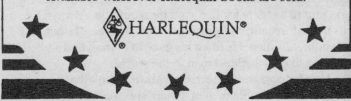

Take 4 bestselling love stories FREE

Plus get a FREE surprise gift!

Special Limited-time Offer

Mail to Harlequin Reader Service®

3010 Walden Avenue
P.O. Box 1867
Buffalo, N.Y. 14240-1867

YES! Please send me 4 free Harlequin Temptation® novels and my free surprise gift. Then send me 4 brand-new novels every month, which I will receive before they appear in bookstores. Bill me at the low price of $3.12 each plus 25¢ delivery and applicable sales tax, if any.* That's the complete price and a savings of over 10% off the cover prices—quite a bargain! I understand that accepting the books and gift places me under no obligation ever to buy any books. I can always return a shipment and cancel at any time. Even if I never buy another book from Harlequin, the 4 free books and the surprise gift are mine to keep forever.

142 HEN CF2M

Name	(PLEASE PRINT)
Address	Apt. No.
City	State	Zip

HARLEQUIN®
Temptation

It's a dating wasteland out there! So what's a girl to do when there's not a marriage-minded man in sight? Go hunting, of course.

Manhunting

Enjoy the hilarious antics of five intrepid heroines, determined to lead Mr. Right to the altar— whether he wants to go or not!

#669 *Manhunting in Memphis—*
Heather MacAllister (February 1998)

#673 *Manhunting in Manhattan—*
Carolyn Andrews (March 1998)

#677 *Manhunting in Montana—*
Vicki Lewis Thompson (April 1998)

#681 *Manhunting in Miami—*
Alyssa Dean (May 1998)

#685 *Manhunting in Mississippi—*
Stephanie Bond (June 1998)

She's got a plan—to find herself a man!

Available wherever Harlequin books are sold.

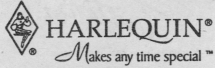